LOW REIGN

LOW REIGN

MARIO D. KING

MDK BOOKS

To Memphis…

One Summer, Two boys—in search of manhood

Growing up is hard to do, especially when you are surrounded by adults who think they know what's best for you in conjunction with the attractive lure of the streets. Lorenzo, Jr. (LJ) & Bee find life in the Low Reign to be exactly like the name indicates but for different reasons.

At 15, LJ longs for the day he can leave home and be rid of his misguided police officer father, his overbearing worrisome mother, and his annoying little brother. Bee wants to be free to pursue his dream of becoming a world-renowned chess player and shed the weight of his alcoholic abusive father, Charles. Charles seems to have drained all the fight out of his battered wife, who is afraid to leave her abuse situation and even more afraid she'll lose Bee to the streets like his older brother. With no one to support their dreams both young men struggle to forge their own path to higher ground where they can reign without question.

During the summer of 1991, in the Low Reign, LJ and Bee finds themselves in a life-altering situation that will shake the fabric of their lives forever during their search for the true meaning of manhood. It's hard to change when you realize what you've been taught about being a man was wrong even if not doing so could cost you everything you have and rob you of what you hoped to be.

ABOUT THE AUTHOR

Mario D. King, born in Memphis, Tennessee, is the author of several books about the complexities of everyday life, including *The Crisis Before Midlife*, *Where Do We Go From Here I* (co-author) and *Where Do We Go From Here II* (co-author). Mario currently lives in North Carolina with his wife and children. Low Reign is the first of three works that he will publish in 2019. Follow @MarioDKing on Instagram and Twitter or visit www.mariodking.com.

This is a work of fiction. Names, characters, places, and incidents either are the product of the author's imagination or are used fictitiously. Any resemblance to actual persons, living or dead, events, or locales is entirely coincidental.

Copyright © 2019 by Mario D. King

All rights reserved. No part of this book may be reproduced or used in any manner without written permission of the copyright owner except for the use of quotations in a book review. For more information, address: MDK Entertainment LLC/ MDK Books, 5931 Sanders Farm Lane, Charlotte, NC, 28216.

First paperback edition August 2019

Book design by Magy1808: Fiverr.com

ISBN 978-0-578-55255-2 (paperback)

www.mariodking.com

CONTENTS

The Devil's Beating His Wife 1

Lessons Wrapped With A Bow 15

Enemy Of My Enemy 28

Dark Clouds 44

The Low Reign Theory 56

Bee's Honey 72

God's Fed Up 88

Scripture On Ice 113

Memphis City Blues 128

The Rising Son..146

Entrapment 164

Freedom 183

THE DEVIL'S BEATING HIS WIFE

Inside his bedroom, the boy sat on the edge of the bed as his eyes worked the room. His face was brown, no longer soft, maturing into its masculinity. With his brows still pinched tight together, overlapping the bridge of his flared nose, he anticipated the day when the four walls that boxed him in would no longer belong to him. It would be the freedom that he'd been longing for—to escape the long arm of his parents' reach. He considered himself to be a man now. His voice had finally caught up with his limbs which had stretched long, leaving behind the once youthful fat that clung to his bones. He was on the cusp of turning sixteen in two months. Manhood was knocking at the door.

It was Saturday morning and that only meant one thing in the Johnson household—it was *clean-up* day. The vibration and echo of the blues music bouncing off the walls, the stench of Comet, Ajax, carpet freshener and Pine-Sol were his alarm clock. Soon his mother would be asking him to grab the bottle of cleaner with the bald white man on the front to scrub down his and his little brother's bathroom. To LJ, browsing underneath the kitchen sink was likened to observing the inside of a mad scientist's laboratory. His mother, Betty, had created all types of cleaning concoctions for every foreseen occasion: instantly remove stubborn stains from clothing, soothe sores from boyish battles, soak up colorful liquids that soiled the carpet, kill unwanted houseguests that snuck in through small cracks in the walls. To LJ, any of those things were better than the smell of bleach. Catching a whiff of bleach was like death to his senses: burning eyes, bitter taste to the tongue, angry nostrils—only his hearing stayed intact. Once, when LJ was younger and had ringworm, his grandmother had told him to grab a cotton swab and the bleach. With his young eyes round as the blue top he held in his hands, LJ waited as his grandmother dabbed his naked skin with the liquid that not only cleaned his clothes, but also sanitized, or "blessed" as his grandmother called it, the house. He often wondered if the white folks he saw on television had to endure such unorthodox unpleasantries. LJ would sulk and believe to himself that there just had to be another remedy for his illnesses besides the "medicines" from underneath the kitchen sink. There weren't many doctor visits in his household, unless it was *really* warranted. The definition of "really" varied: not just a dislocated finger, but the bone had to be protruding from the skin, not just a common cold, but you had to be in the second stages of the flu. However, in due time, his ailments would miraculously be cleared. He learned to never question his grandmother again. Like his mother, she was a magician to their circumstances.

"LJ," his mother yelled. Her voice magically overpowered the bass and riffs from the music that breathed life into the small ranch house in the heart of Whitehaven. The lyrics from the song were sung by a man, painfully describing the three people sleeping in his bed: he, his woman and the man in his woman's head—now *ain't* that the blues? LJ's mother's voice was soft, sweet, mesmerizing. To an outsider, one may mistakenly take her to be some type of pushover or one to be taken lightly. LJ and those closest to her knew otherwise. The elegant tone that tickled LJ's ears was nothing more than a mask to him. They knew the vile and demonstrative secrets of her tongue that she would unleash when provoked. But it all came from a place of love.

One recent Saturday, he had decided to test his newly found manhood as he was a ripe fifteen-year-old boy prepping to turn the big one-six. When his mother flicked on the light and told him to wake up and get to it, the boldness and bass from his youthful mouth blurted out, "Will you please turn off my light and get out?" When darkness blanketed his room and she closed the door, you could see the bravado within his chest leap from his soon-to-be-manly body as if it glowed. The strength and courage of his words hung over his head like a halo. The aura was magnificent. It was a small victory to him. Maybe there was something to this thing called manhood after all. No sooner was he championing his slight victory, with his sniggering mouth and dancing toes underneath the warmth of his sheets, than he heard his door swing open violently, slamming into his desk, causing a small dent to form on the door, underneath the doorknob. He then felt the wrath and sting of some of the consequences of being an adult. Life had a way of still bruising your ass no matter how grown you thought you'd become, and his mother's hand was like that of God throwing down a lightning bolt. She was life.

Now standing with his arms limp at his sides, boxer shorts moist from the heat within the linen, uneven on his thighs, bare chested without a hint of hair, he sighed as he began to drag his naked feet over the carpeted floor. There were clothes strewn about any and every place: over the arms of a chair, on the floor, on the edge of a hamper, on his desk. The controller from his video game console dangled from the back of the oak chair made from the hands of his grandfather, the cord snaked around its leg. A bowl with a spoon and milk residue sat atop his desk. It was accompanied by scattered basketball cards of the unknown players he didn't want to add to his collection of the popular players which were inside the black binder that he kept void of dust—the only clean item in his room. A wire hanger was wedged inside the top of the closet door and frame, stretched out wide and round like the rim of a basketball hoop. A poster of Magic Johnson covered the closet door. LJ picked up a pair of socks that were folded into the perfect ball and shot it toward the homemade hoop as he mouthed and fantasized, "LJ for threeeee."

"*LJ,* did you hear me calling you?"

"No ma'am," he lied.

His mother stood underneath the door frame, plastic gloves on her hands, rollers in her hair, robe swallowing her body whole. Her morning face was as beautiful as her evening. Betty's complexion was that of cinnamon. Her eyes were cat-like, amber in color. Her hair, when unrolled, was a free-flowing bundle of long, bouncing curls that hung down to the middle of her back. People would often ask her where she was from or what she was mixed with. When she'd tell them Memphis and black, she got enjoyment out of seeing their eyes dance from embarrassment.

"Look at this damn room. Makes no sense. I just don't understand sometimes."

It's not meant for you to understand are the words that twirled within LJ's head as he checked to be sure she didn't have a belt in hand. Three years earlier he'd told his mother that very thing when he'd heard the song titled "Parents Just Don't Understand" by DJ Jazzy Jeff & The Fresh Prince. One Christmas, LJ's father had purchased a VCR for the family, and he couldn't wait to record his favorite hip-hop videos. The first one was "Parents Just Don't Understand." He played the song so much that it began to playback distorted and he would smack the television as if it was to blame. Like magic, it often would work. Maybe he too was a magician in training.

"Where did you and Bee go last night? I called over to his house and Tammy said that y'all weren't there."

LJ knew that a lie could only travel so far, and his mother would soon find it, but he wasn't ready to willingly unlock the mystery for her. She had to work to crack this code. Especially if it would lead to him being punished.

"Momma we *was* there."

Now standing in the room within breathing distance from LJ, the top of her head stopping where his lips started, as she arched her chin up, she said, "So she lying?"

LJ knew better than to fall for the trap. There were certain rules and things that you just didn't do in his household. One of those things was to call an adult a liar. You couldn't even utter the word 'lie.' Saying that word was like stealing tithes from the collection plate at church. A lying thieving heathen is what you would be.

Stepping back to a more comfortable distance from his mother as if she was a foreigner intruding on his personal space, he replied, "I ain't sayin' that."

"So, what *are* you saying then?"

"I'on know. I just know we was there." He knew he had to think of something quick to stop the full court press his mother was applying. "Maybe she didn't know we was in the backyard. I *bet* you she didn't know that. *You* can call and ask Bee yourself if you wanna."

She too was to wise for that trick. She knew that he and Bee had already drafted the lies they would tell to hide their tracks. She continued to take mental notes, because she knew in due time the boy who still had milk on his breath would soon burp up the information she wanted.

"Well I'm just telling you this: Don't ask me about no money for no movies and skating ring if this room, y'all's bathroom *and* that kitchen ain't clean."

In the living room, a hyper nine-year-old boy was slamming a pillow against the cushions of the floral-patterned couch. He was mimicking the moves of one of the professional wrestlers that was triumphing over his opponent on the television set which was sitting atop the bigger mahogany television set that no longer worked. The boy, Robert—nicknamed Robbie—slung his championship belt, made from old vinyl album covers and covered with duct and electrical tape, over his shoulder as he'd won the match. Standing tall atop the couch and triumphant in his own right, he was about to give his victory speech when he heard the voice of another foe in his presence. His wrestling eyes, sharp and narrow, shifted toward the villain now standing near the coffee table, dressed in a blue robe with a crown of pink rollers atop her head.

"Boy, if you don't get your ends off my couch like that—"

"Okay Mama," the champ replied, gracefully and quickly bowing out to a formidable opponent stronger than he.

"Take that stuff outside if you want to jump around. I've told you several times that this is not your personal playground or wrestling ring."

"Okay Mama," Robbie said as he darted toward the door.

"Uhm where are *you* going?"

"Outside like you just said," Robbie replied with confusion on his face.

"Not with them clothes on you're not. You better go put on your play clothes."

Robbie looked down at the outfit he'd worn to school the day before. The shirt was stained from the spaghetti that he'd eaten. With a perplexed look set on his face, he replied, "But it's dirty already."

"That's what the washing machine is for. Take them off and put them in the pile in the hall. Make sure you put them in the right color pile too. But before you do that, get the spray in that green bottle I got under the sink and spray that shirt. That stain will be good and gone 'bout the time I get through with it," she said with a confident curl to her lips.

"Why *he* don't got to clean up?" LJ asked, standing in the opening of the kitchen. His father's slippers were on his feet, but his feet were not yet long enough to fill them. He despised the fact that the little trouble-starter didn't hold his fair share of the responsibilities, the same as he. When LJ was his age, he wasn't afforded the luxury of skipping out on Saturday morning clean-up days to go play outside with his friends.

"LJ need to worry about LJ," his mother replied.

With a quick flick of his tongue like a hissing snake, Robbie gestured with his hands that he was wearing the belt of champions and walked down the hall, leaping over piles and slapping hands with his imaginary fans congratulating him on yet another victory.

Inside the bathroom, LJ had a t-shirt wrapped around his nose and mouth protecting himself from the strong fumes of the green powder that was awaiting him inside the slightly stained white tub. "I hate when she does this," he whispered. The wallpaper was a colorful assortment of yellows, orange and green. Over the toilet hung a picture of a young boy facing his own toilet with the following words hovering over it: *"If you sprinkle when you tinkle, be a sweetie and wipe the seatie."* As LJ scrubbed the tub, he reminisced on the night before when his tongue slow danced with a girl's tongue two blocks away from where he was supposed to be. He anticipated doing it again, envisioning letting his hands touch and massage places that were only reserved for the cool. His manhood began to heat and swell within his boxers.

In the living room, Betty was peering through the blinds at Robbie and some friends taking turns putting their ears against the cracks of the concrete in the driveway as the rain tapped against their youthful frames. She knew they were listening for the sound of the devil beating his wife. It was a tale that resonated in the south during sun-showers. The rain is said to be the devil's wife's tears. She wished her magic allowed her to keep her boy's youthful innocence. As with LJ, she wanted her grip to keep them from the unforgiving streets that awaited them, as she knew the streets' eyes were always watching and those eyes would shed no tears or blink twice. Breaking her gaze was the sight of a police car pulling into her driveway. Her heart accelerated.

Stepping out of the vehicle, the policeman rubbed the top of Robbie's head and held small conversations with Robbie's friends. Betty smiled at the cop as he approached the front door. She was relieved as her husband, Officer Johnson, arrived home safe and sound from protecting in his own way not just his family, but the city's citizens from the streets.

Three houses down, Bee was slouched in a bean bag playing a game of chess against himself. As he maneuvered and flopped about, trying to find a position that was more comfortable, small white beads shot out from multiple holes in the bean bag. It was unable to hold its shape like it once had. Soon there would be no use for it.

There was no clean-up Saturdays in his household. No annoying little brothers or sisters to complain about. It was just he, his mother and part-time father. His room was neat to LJ's sloppiness. He only had the essentials: bed, dresser, garbage can. No video game consoles, or posters of idolized basketball gods covered his walls. However, to him, he had everything he needed—a chessboard.

He'd learned to play chess one summer when he had to go stay with his paternal grandparents in Jackson, Mississippi due to his mother's work schedule. His grandfather, Willie Earl, used to take him by the barbershop to teach him two things: how to cut hair and play chess. He'd always told him with those two things he would be able to either make some money or have peace of mind. Through a voice that was seasoned and eyes that were wise, he would continue, "A man that don't have money in his pocket or the 'bility to make it and can't find sommin' to keep his head straight will be pulled to do the wrong thangs in life. Lissen to me boy." It was his grandfather that nicknamed him Bee; his government name is Brandon. His grandfather was surprised at how quickly his understudy was able to pick up the game of chess. "You got a sharp mind boy. Almost like a bee. Somebody play you for a fool if they wanna. You turn around and sting they ass sommin' real good, I tell ya." Amid the laughter within the barbershop, Brandon—now Bee—reveled in the encouragement and exuberance that lived within that tiny shop. In due time, he was beating ol' Shifty-Eyes Kenny in a friendly game of chess. Kenny got the name "Shifty-Eyes" by his keen ability to allow only one of his eyes to roam toward another woman while the other stayed focused on his wife. At least, that's according to the locals. Bee always marveled at the man that stood before him. So much wisdom. So much guidance. Every wrinkle upon his face, clear of blemishes, represented a story seen by his eyes and told from his tongue. With his hands, not steady as they once were, he painted an abstract for his grandson in the form of a bee. The painting, along with an old chess piece, was the last physical gift he'd received from his grandfather, but the gift of the secrets of life was the gift that kept on giving.

Now at the age of fifteen, Bee knew that he was one of, if not, *the* best chess player in the world. Unfortunately, no one in his immediate surroundings and circles of influence knew how to play the game, at least not well enough to test him. Like LJ, he couldn't wait for his manhood to arrive so he could go to a place where he could compete against the people he had once seen on a news program about chess tournaments.

Still sitting, he was disturbed by an all-too-familiar sound across the hall. He stood and walked to the door, slamming it shut tight. He was trying to protect his ears from the sound. The sound of the devil beating his wife.

LESSONS WRAPPED WITH A BOW

L J hurdled over the muddy puddle as he approached the steps to the front door. The steady pour had come to an end. The aftermath left the type of mugginess in the air that made your skin feel as if musk was seeping into your pores. Mosquitos, the size of cats some would exaggerate, swarmed around waiting to taste the blood of the locals. Sweating profusely, LJ wiped the top of his forehead with the back of his hand. He tugged at the collar of his t-shirt, in hopes of catching a hint of a cool draft. Instead, all that returned was the odor of his cologne and the whiff of body heat that was trapped within his shirt.

He took cautious steps up the porch, avoiding the large dip in the concrete. Standing atop it, he glanced at the unkempt yard full of overgrown weeds. To his right was an empty cooler filled with rain, which made LJ think of the dirty bath water his little brother always left for him to drain. As he turned his head to his left, he saw an assortment of empty potato chip bags, candy wrappers and an empty Styrofoam cup decorating the neglected flowerbed. LJ giggled once his eyes caught the cup. He knew it had to be Bee's, because it was chewed down to the middle. That's how Bee liked to eat his freeze cups.

Before knocking at the door, he lowered his head toward his white sneakers to check for any blemishes. He cringed at the sight of the mud that was caked up in the cracks of the sole and the sides. He prayed that it was not dog shit. He broke off a stick from a scraggy bush and attempted to surgically remove the brown clumps from his soles, only to leaving behind a trail of smudgy stains. He aggressively slid his feet across the towel that was in front of the door, eyes narrowed, brows pinched, nose flared. In the glass door, he was able to catch a glimpse of his appearance: oversized t-shirt, colorful shorts that extended well below his knees, almost kissing the tops of his socks. He noticed that his father's features were starting to become more distinct. When he was younger and still had a baby face, it was his mother's face that he saw. As his face began to take shape, more defined by a stronger jawline and beads of hair sprouting on his upper lip, it was now his father's face that he saw—brown and handsome.

"Come on in, LJ. Bee is in the back," Tammy said as she clutched her silky robe tight against her petite frame. Her eyes, once large and embraced the richness of life, had since been dulled and voided of it. Her cheeks used to rise to the bottoms of her eyes when LJ visited. Now she welcomed LJ with the shame that had become a permanent attribute of her face. An attribute that included the left side of her face being a darker shade of red at the cheek, puffiness to the eye, and a bulge at the lip.

LJ had never asked or said anything to Bee about it and Bee had never offered an invitation to discuss it. Soon, LJ began to realize that such bruises only appeared when the old burgundy car that was long in the back was in the driveway or under the carport. There were times when LJ would skip over Bee's house and go visit another friend when he saw the car in the driveway, but as their bond grew stronger and more mature as friends, he began to sense that Bee needed him there. Even though their lips never allowed the words to escape, LJ understood.

Inside the living room, a red loveseat with white circles was covered in plastic. It was adjacent to a grandfather clock that peaked nearly at the ceiling. For fellow Memphians, everything in life seemed to always be just shy of reaching the top and the clock was a good representation of it. LJ had never seen the round gold pendulum inside the clock move or make a sound. It was like a treasured jewel, not recognizing or living out its purpose. It could have been part of a piece of jewelry, on the wrist, around the neck or on the finger of someone wealthy, but there it was, stuck inside an old piece of wood. Nobody ever told it the value it had or about the treasure of the antique wood that housed it. It was a keen representation of the people in the city.

Ash trays with several cigarette butts, some with red lipstick at the end, covered the coffee table. One was still lit, on its last leg, trying to hold on to what was left of its flame before the burn was gone, leaving behind a curl of smoke fading.

LJ walked past the framed photographs of Bee, his mother and his father looking like the Huxtables in their colorful sweaters and wide smiles. Like the current state of Tammy's face, photographs tend to be distorted in view at times. While they can be memories trapped in time, they can also be figments of one's imagination—a lie within a frame.

Inside Bee's bedroom, Bee asked with welcoming eyes, "Your mom's finally let you out of the house?"

"Mane, I thought she would never let me out. You know how she get. I'm glad she finally started watching her stories that I recorded. That's the only way I was able to get out of there." The two of them locked eyes before they said in unison, "Who shot J.R.? Who shot J.R.?" They both laughed as LJ continued, "People been going crazy over that show since its coming to an end. I don't know what my mom's gonna do with herself now."

Bee was still in his bean bag. His shirt was swallowing his adolescent body whole, but he filled his out a little more than LJ did. A pillow slip was atop the bed with shaven hair scattered about next to a set of clippers. LJ removed the box of curl activator from inside the blue milk crate and flipped the crate over.

"You can go grab a chair from the kitchen, nigga. You know the drill."

"I'm good. I'm cool with sitting right here," LJ replied.

Sitting on the floor, legs extended, one ankle over the other, right arm resting on the milk crate they took from school last week, LJ asked, "Any word about tonight?" He was now rubbing his hands together; his face couldn't hide the excitement.

"Mane, I don't have enough money to go to the movies." Bee reached for the blinds at his window and lifted three of them up with two fingers. "I would go see if I could cut a yard or wash a car or something, but the rain messed that up. How much money *you* got?" Looking out into the streets, Bee's eyes glanced over the yard that was three weeks behind in getting trimmed. He used to think about how the rain nourished the soil, bringing to life all the beauty that sprouted up to the world—lush grass, trees, flowers. However, with all that beauty, it also birthed the weeds, which would often overpower the beauty, bringing an ugliness to it that illuminated the necessity to have balance in life. The weeds served a purpose as well: pulling up water and nutrients, providing food, controlling insects. Bee often wondered if he was a flower or a weed. Did it even matter?

LJ pulled out a wrinkled ten-dollar bill from his pocket. "This should be enough for us to get in and play a couple of games at the arcade."

"That's cool, but what about the girls? You know they go want us to pay they way too."

LJ sighed as he dropped his head. No longer smiling. "Damn, you right about that. I would ask my dad for another ten, but he be trippin' sometimes.

"Your dad be too busy trying to lock people up." Bee laughed and continued, "I'm just trippin', fool. But for real though, you ever think about why your dad wanted to be a cop?"

LJ hunched his shoulders. Earlier that spring, the world had witnessed the brutal beating of Rodney King by the LAPD. Thousands of miles away from California, the south had always had a fractured and tumultuous relationship with the police. There was no trust. There was no relationship. Through Jim Crow eyes the relationship with the police and the community was an authoritative contract that was forged not in favor of the people. LJ often wondered why his dad would willingly want to be the enemy of his people, his neighborhood—his son. A confusion lingered within his mind, an inner battle that conflicted with his beliefs. His father had never shied away from telling his boys about the ugliness behind the politics and the harsh realities of his line of work. When his father walked into his home after his duty, he would often say, "Thank you Lord for allowing me to make it home." He would then tell Betty, LJ and Robbie about some of the "truths" of some of "their people." Truths that the neighborhood voluntarily stayed blind to.

When Lorenzo didn't wear the blue uniform and badge, he was a husband and a father. But above all, he was a man. A hardworking man, and a man of the neighborhood, nevertheless. He watched sports and wrestling, drank beer and partied no different than the other men in the neighborhood, but when he put on that uniform, it was as if all his cool had been stripped away from him and he instantly became one of *them*. As he tenured in the unit, even LJ couldn't tell on which side of the fence his father stood. He asked him about the Rodney King beating and his dad replied, "We don't know what happened prior. Don't judge. Wait on the facts and details before siding with anything." Those weren't the words LJ's *fight the power* ears wanted to hear. LJ was disappointed. It was at that moment that he had wanted to rush into manhood, so he could be the man he thought his father wasn't.

Seeing the uneasiness in LJ's demeanor, Bee said, "You know I'm just clowning. You want to go sit outside on the porch? I'm really trying to get up out this house before Charles wake up. One day mane—" He shook his head and twisted his mouth in such a way to mask the hurt and hatred that was built up inside.

Outside, LJ and Bee sat under the carport, looking out into the street that was full of their most intimate childhood memories. That street was their home as much as the brick and wood where they rested their heads at night. It was on that street where he, Bee and a couple of other friends would race cigarette butts down the drain. They would start at Mrs. Moore's house that had the huge oak tree in the front and follow the butts as they traveled the path of the flood of rain or running water from someone washing their car, finessing through leaves and other debris. Not all the butts made it to the end of the drain, but that was the point of the game. Only one was to survive making it to the drain to be washed away in another layer of the unknown trail of the sewer. Game of life.

The sky was still a dull gray. It looked as if no clouds were in the sky. Leaning on the steel bumper of his father's car, Bee asked, "What time you think your mom will be able to drop us off?"

LJ hunched his shoulders. "I can't wait to get some wheels. You don't want to just catch a ride from Travis and them?"

Bee stared off into space for a minute before replying. He shook his head. "I don't know, mane. They be getting into too much shit now." The "shit" Bee was referring to was selling drugs and fighting. The week before, Travis and some of their other childhood friends got into a huge altercation at the skating rink that left one young boy shot in the arm, others with bruised faces and shoes being removed from the feet of their targets. It all started when Travis contorted his fingers into a sign that was disrespectful to a group of people standing across from them. Bee and LJ ended up being bystanders to the chaos, but it was now a chaos of normalcy—a product of their environment.

"That fool do be on it, but that may be our only way there. My mom ain't gonna wanna make that drive because Robbie got some birthday party to go to. Besides, if my mom took us, she would be trying to make us watch *The Five Heartbeats* or some shit like that. I'm trying to see *New Jack City*. And my dad...well, I ain't trying to roll up anywhere in that police car."

"A car is a car. At least *you* can ask your dad! Charles would see us walking and wouldn't even offer. If he did, he would take that ten dollars you got in your pocket." He shook his head and twisted his mouth again before continuing, "I heard *Five Heartbeats* was good though. I'm cool watching it if we have too." He threw a rock toward the street, watching it skip as if it was against a river.

LJ leaned up on his toes. "If the ground wasn't so wet, we could have gone over to Red's crib and hooped," LJ said as he demonstrated his best jump shot.

"For what? You're slaw anyway," Bee joked and jumped pretending to block the imaginary ball from LJ's hand.

"You ever figure out what you gonna do about getting into some of those tournaments you be talkin' 'bout?" LJ asked.

"For chess?"

"Yeah nigga. I shole wasn't talking about basketball."

"I don't know, mane. I mean, don't nobody really be up on chess in Memphis like that."

"I'm sure it's some places around here. We just got to find it."

"It *ain't* around here. Probably in those white neighborhoods. They ain't trying to teach niggas chess around here."

"Why you like that junt so much?"

"Same reason why you like basketball." He paused and stared into space. "Besides, I done already told you—my grandad taught me and I'm really good at the shit."

At the corner, a blue car with a white top eased past the stop sign. The windows were dark, and the system was loud, rattling the trunk to a vibrating rhythm.

"What you li'l niggas trying to get into?"

LJ looked at Bee with pleading eyes. Bee slightly shook his head before dropping it toward the ground.

"Come on fool," LJ whispered with a convincing desperation in his tone.

Bee sighed and whispered back, "I still ain't got no *money*."

Now maneuvering toward the car, LJ whispered, "I got you fool—fuck it, let's roll."

Knowing that he couldn't disappoint LJ, Bee reluctantly let out a, "Fuck it," in return.

Sometimes lessons come packaged as a gift wrapped with a bow. In the comfort of Travis' car, they told him what they had planned, and they were off to the sounds of a heavy bass-laden track with a fast flow tiptoeing over the beat. A cloud of smoke lingered over their heads; the smell was sour yet sweet. A wad of bills held together with three rubber bands lay in the center of the front row. An uneasiness was settling within Bee. He wondered if it was the same uneasiness his brother felt before he journeyed on his path of no return. Life doesn't always allow you the opportunity to grow from the lessons you've learned. Especially if you didn't have control over the life that you didn't choose.

ENEMY OF MY ENEMY

A rainbow arched over the building with big blue letters that read 'Southbrook Mall' stretched wide and lengthy across the top. LJ, leaning back in the passenger seat, head resting comfortably against the headrest, eyes fixated on the roof, took his last pull from the marijuana joint that Travis had rolled up. With his eyes now closed, LJ allowed the cannabis to do its job as the smoke hovered over his face like a drifting cloud. His senses began to relax. A sudden tightness in his head squeezed his worries away, allowing the effect to trickle to his heart, causing it to accelerate. When he attempted to open his eyes, he noticed that his lids were heavier than he last remembered. He giggled. When he turned his head and glanced at Travis, who was smoking the last remains of the roach joint, LJ could hear it burn as Travis took multiple puffs, his lips puckered as if he was leaning in for a kiss. When LJ looked out the window toward the sky, he didn't see a rainbow that consisted of the seven colors of the spectrum. In his altered mind, they were streaks of broken colors bending to the light, trying to find their way—possibly in pursuit of that pot of gold that supposedly lay on the other side. He began to wonder why only one end of the color spectrum was privy enough to get to the pot, when it was the full cast of the rainbow that made it beautiful. The aftermath of the weed was robbing him of his logic and tapping his pockets for anything else that remained of his common sense.

Stepping out of the car, LJ—with his eyelids now stiff and too heavy for his eyes to be at full bloom—giggled at the satisfaction of his feet touching the ground. Each step felt heavy as if he would contribute to the abundance of potholes that covered the asphalt. His legs were excavation machines. He giggled again as he ironed his shirt with his hands, trying to smooth out every wrinkle. "My mom would kill me if she seen these wrinkles," he mumbled. Marijuana's cousin paranoia was paying him a visit.

"Nigga, why you always giggling?" Travis asked. Travis released the latch to the driver's seat, leaning it forward, allowing Bee to exit from the back. Travis stood in his blue khaki shorts that stopped just above his knees and designer t-shirt. A gold chain that glistened when the light hit it right hung heavy on his neck. He had two shiny gold teeth in his left and right laterals.

His entire frame was long and lanky at the limbs, with his forearms being an awkward length to his upper arms, like a character in an Ernie Barnes' painting. It didn't take much of a lean for his knuckles to graze the ground when he shot dice. "I told you not to hit the bud. You should have done like my nigga Bee and stayed away from it."

Travis reached and grabbed his wad of cash and stuffed it on the inside of his shorts. Bee cut his eyes in Travis' direction. He'd always considered him to be a man amongst boys. He was a mentor of sorts, teaching Bee the way of the streets. Bee and Travis had become friends in the third grade. Travis, having been held back twice, was more mature than his wet-behind-the-ears peers. On one occasion, Travis had educated Bee on how many holes a girl had inside her vagina and what it looked like. He also showed Bee how to shoot dice and smoke a cigarette—"man lessons" as Travis often called them. Soon these "man lessons" became "real nigga shit" and Travis schooled him on those as well. When they reached the sixth grade, a rumor had been circulating that Travis had had sex with one of the teachers. He neither approved nor denied the claim. His folklore carried over into junior high school. When he dropped out of school in the ninth grade, his peers teased him about how he was spending more time at school than when he was officially enrolled. Travis felt he was wasting his time as he already felt years behind in terms of creating the type of life that consisted of him obtaining a diploma or college degree. He and his teachers had convinced him that he would have to "make it" on his own terms, own rules, by taking his own path. It's a path that had been traveled by many feet before him, but it's a path where the journey was shorter, and the destination varied, often detouring to a one-way street or dead-end.

Staring at his beeper, Travis said, "Ant and Freddie should be on their way too." He focused his attention on Bee and asked, "How you gonna have a fresh curl and still not be able to get no pussy?"

LJ laughed at the accusation. As he slapped hands with Travis, he said, "You right about that."

Bee didn't laugh. Sitting on the hood of the car, he squinted to protect his eyes from the sun that had just broken from behind the darkness of a cloud. He said, "I need to find a job when school get out." The sight of the wad of cash Travis was holding—in addition to him depending on LJ to pay his way into the movies *and* arcade—pulled at his pride and boyish ego. Bee had learned over the years that the people who you depended upon are often the ones who tend to hurt you the most. To him, dependency equated to control, and he refused to be a dependent. Not to family. Not to friends. Not to women. And especially not to a system that was designed for him to fail. Like Travis, he had to make a way out of his own way. Since his grandfather had passed, there'd been no voice of reason or feet who had walked the path that he was destined to journey. He was on his own.

"Shit, I wish I *would* look for a job!" Travis replied with a facial expression that expressed the disdain and absurdity of the statement. "Nigga, we just got *out* of a recession and you over here talking about getting a *job*. Doing what? Bagging groceries, handing niggas they roller-skate or taking food *orders*? Fuck that."

With his arms wrapped around his knees pulled toward his chest, Bee hung his head down and let his saliva fall in a long spiraling drool toward the asphalt. LJ jumped atop the hood to join him, only to stretch his limbs with his high eyes looking toward the sky. "I haven't even thought about none of the shit y'all talking about. What the fuck is a recession anyway?"

"It's when the economy—" Travis shook his head and continued, "You li'l niggas stupid. One can't handle his high and the other one on some sad man shit. Get off my ride and let's gone in here to at least see what the deal is."

As LJ, Bee and Travis walked in, two adolescents, who appeared to be the same age as them, were being escorted out of the mall in handcuffs by two police officers. One officer was black and the other white. A small crowd had formed near one of the entrance doors where some kids were jeering and laughing. "That nigga said plop," said a boy who seemed to be too young to be amongst the other kids. "Yeah, he straight sprung on that mane," said another as he smashed his fist into the open palm of his other hand, giving his best reenactment to the thrill of the crowd.

During the commotion there was a man standing idle near the corner of the entrance mumbling to himself. He was dressed unseasonably warm in his jeans which were long in the legs, the excess overlapping the shoes one couldn't even see. A red coat was draped over his shoulder, covering the long-sleeved shirt he wore. Unkempt coils sprouted from his head, magnifying a face that resembled a motherless child's. As they approached, he extended his arm toward Travis. Travis stared at the plastic cup that jingled to the tune of loose change as the man shook it. No sooner than when the cup was in his reach did Travis pull out his wad of cash and fill the cup with five ten-dollar bills and nod toward the man.

LJ slid his hand in one of his pockets and pulled out a couple of coins. "I'm about to run to the pay phone real quick," he said.

"Mane, you could have gave that change to that dude over there. You about to block yo' blessings fool," Travis replied with a chuckle.

"And what would that blessing be?" LJ asked, his eyes still heavy. "You sound like my grandma, talking 'bout some blessings. I hope I'm *blessed* with Krystal coming through," LJ replied with a sneaky grin.

As LJ walked to the pay phone, Travis nudged Bee on the shoulder. "Yo, what's up with you?" he asked.

Bee turned toward Travis with a rather stoic look about his eyes as he replied, "What you mean?"

"You been acting kind of funny lately."

"Funny how?"

Travis twisted his mouth as he replied, "I'on know. I can't really explain it, but it's like you been zoned out or something."

Bee didn't respond.

Travis with his pearls for eyes stopped and laid his hand atop Bee's right shoulder. "Ain't nobody fucking with you is it? Remember—yo' enemy is my enemy. Fo' life, right?"

Bee shook his head. "Naw. It ain't nothing like that."

"Well, what is it then nigga?" Travis asked with curiosity in his eyes.

"It ain't nothing mane."

Travis sighed. "Aite then—I ain't gonna press you on it. Just know if you need to holla at someone, I got yo' back. You still know that right?"

Bee nodded.

"You still fucking with that chess shit?"

Bee's eyes lit up as he replied, "All day. That ain't gonna never change."

"Dig that then." He proceeded to hand Bee some of the money from his wad.

"What's this for? You know I can't take this." He attempted to give it back, but Travis pushed his hand away.

"You my nigga, ain't you? If I got it, you got it! What's understood ain't always got to be said. You take that, don't even worry about the payback." Travis looked back toward the direction where LJ was and continued, "Dude down there begging for them broads to come and shit."

Bee slid the money deep into his pockets, hoping that he wouldn't regret the exchange. His eyes roamed back toward the man in the corner and he could only imagine the pain of having to empty out your pockets of ego, only to have your vulnerability and gratitude to give in return.

Inside the arcade, a boy whose shirt was tight around his belly and overlapped his belt was leaning against one of the machines. His fade was uneven and shabby. His face was circular, but his forehead was flat. His shorts seemed to be two sizes too tight in the waist. "I had her legs like this," he said.

Travis twisted his mouth as he replied, "Nigga quit *lying*."

Still demonstrating the vulgar act, the young man replied, "I *swear* before *God*. Tell em' Ant." The young man's name was Freddie. Freddie's upbringing would seem horrific to some. He'd never met his parents, at least as he could remember. He'd been in the care of the foster system for most of his life. His paternal grandparents had taken him in last summer. It was that or the juvenile court system. It would have been another last name in the family tree in the hands of the system. His hand-me-down clothing always seemed to be two to three sizes too small, usually due to his unhealthy eating habits. He carried a distinct odor due to a combination of bad hygiene practices and no consistent running water. Kids used to tease him about his afflictions and mishaps, until he learned the art of punching a kid in the face. He also realized that he could use comedy and cracking jokes as a defense mechanism. He knew he could beat you with either his hands or mouth. Sometimes both. He now wore a new confidence that fit him like the snug shirt that melted to his belly.

LJ retuned to the arcade in company of three young ladies. He was holding hands with one who was the color of sand. Her hair draped over one of her shoulders, while the front looked like an oversized bun. Her eyes sparkled like shells against the shore. When she smiled, you could see a hint of braces illuminating the nakedness of her mouth. Her name was Krystal.

The other two girls went to the same school as he and Bee. Jacqueline was tall and flat chested. She was not only underdeveloped physically, but mentally as well. She still had an innocent immaturity at the age of sixteen. Nevertheless, Bee still had an adoration for her. She was dark-skinned like himself. Her hair was straight like his mother's. LaWanda was a year behind them, but she was the first to lose her virginity. Her body curved like a woman's—the type they'd seen in the magazines that were hid atop the bathroom cabinet at Bee's house. Her lips were always the butt of a sexual rumor or joke. She adored the attention. She sought out the validation to mask the insecurity she had about her nose. In its unique beauty, she despised the shape and girth of it, feeling uncomfortable in unfamiliar places. Therefore, if they decided to focus on her body and not her hideous nose, which was beautiful, she was okay with that. She was fifteen.

"The movie starts in fifteen minutes. Y'all ready to roll up in there?" LJ asked.

The boys all looked at each other as they sized up the young ladies standing before them. There were four of them and only two girls left as LJ had already stamped his claim for Krystal. Ant approached Jacqueline and reached to grab her hand. "Jackie, you looking good over there. I see you all fly in your gangsta' Nikes and shit." She blushed at his confidence.

Travis made his move for the other girl. "Your name LaWanda, ain't it?" She nodded. "I remember you."

She looked at Travis and replied, "You should remember me."

"Why is that?" Travis replied, opening his eyes wide with a curl of the mouth, his gold teeth becoming the focal point of his attractiveness.

"Don't *act* like you don't remember," LaWanda said with a twirl of the neck. She puckered her lips, crossing her arms against her chest.

Travis looked in his boys' direction and smiled at his ignorance. "Remember what?"

"You grabbed my ass!"

"I grabbed your *what*? *How*? Y'all just got here."

"Don't play." She returned a smile. "You don't remember when you and that stupid friend of yours was playing that game y'all used to play. I can't remember the name, but it was when you couldn't open your hand until you touched a girl's booty, but if you opened it before then you were gay."

Travis started to laugh hysterically. "Girl that *shit* was like in elementary."

"*And*? I still remember," she replied. Her arms were still crossed, but her eyes were more welcoming than they had been.

Travis extended his hand to hers and guided her toward him. He began to whisper into her ear. She giggled. She playfully slapped him on the arm. She laughed. He whispered some more. She hit him again and giggled.

Bee and Freddie looked on awkwardly as they were the only two without a date to the movie. "Man, *fuck* the movies. Let's go do something else," Freddie blurted out. "I seen this shit already anyway," he lied. "I got my grandma's car," he continued trying to impress the girls. "And Travis you got yours too, right?"

Travis nodded.

"Let's ride up to Libertyland or something. The movies be boring as fuck," Freddie added.

They all looked around, searching each other's faces.

"My parents ain't about to come back out this way to pick us up and then take us to Libertyland." Jaqueline rebutted.

"We'll take y'all," Travis replied.

"But we told them we would be here," LaWanda added.

"I know. Here is what you do." Freddie went on to tell them to call their parents and lie that the movie had a delay and it would be over later than expected. He went on to assure the girls that they would be back well before their parents would return to pick them up.

LJ and Krystal had walked away for some privacy as the group decided on their plans. Standing outside, LJ and Krystal held hands as he leaned against a post near the main entrance.

"You know we can just stay here if you want to," he said.

She sighed. "I know that, *but* when your friends make up their minds, what can you do?" Krystal replied as she chewed on her gum.

"I'm glad you came," he said. His eyes were locked with hers. He could feel the heat of his passion rising within his chest. His high was coming down.

"My dad is coming home soon," she said.

"*Word*? He was in that war, right?"

"Yup."

"You know what's crazy?" LJ asked.

"What?"

"You know my dad the police—*right*?"

"Yeah. *And*? So what?"

"I'm just saying like—your dad was over there fighting. My dad be here fighting. *We* be out here fighting each other. It's like—who the real enemy?"

She continued to listen while holding his hand before they were interrupted by the sound of a body smashing against the door. They both jerked and maneuvered away from the door. Freddie was holding a youth by the collar with one hand while he punched his face with the other. Another boy grabbed Freddie by the neck and began to pull him off, his arm squeezing tighter with each aggressive tug. Ant and Travis began to punch and kick with precision. LJ pulled away from Krystal as she shouted for them to stop. LJ's hand met the jaw of another boys. Bee looked on at the ruckus before him from the inside of the mall. Under the microscope of it all, it was meaningless. It was a means to a path that was only paved to be a one-way street. Bee needed an alternate route. But he decided to join in the chaos. After all, the money in his pocket was burning a hole in his conscious. It was that type of control that he feared that led him to walk out that door. In that moment, he saw what looked like black steel rise in the hands of another kid. The sound was deafening. Bodies began to scatter and drop. Screams from girls. Tough talk from boys. Cries from others. It wasn't long before another set of flashing blue and red lights surrounded the mall and the enemy of an enemy appeared.

DARK CLOUDS

LJ remembered the first time his father pulled into the driveway in his new vehicle. It was an oddity to his eyes. The intensity of the blue and red lights flashing before him instinctively made him want to flee. His skinny legs wobbled and bucked as they positioned for a runner's pose. LJ had just turned twelve and he had already been conditioned that those flashing blue and red lights weren't a sign of protection and servitude. Amused that he'd startled his oldest son, Lorenzo laughed as he stepped out of the vehicle. He stood tall as a proud smile spread across his face, exposing a set of teeth usually reserved for advertisements. The dark blue uniform was complementary against his dark skin, but something felt odd, almost wrong in LJ's eyes when he saw his father as Officer Johnson for the first time.

"Well, come on boys—come have a look," his father said as he leaned against the hood. Still smiling, he tilted his hat in the direction of his wife and continued,

"I may have to arrest you ma'am." She blushed as she stared into the eyes of the handsome officer before her and replied, "And for what crime, may I ask?"

"You're a thief ma'am—from the moment I first met you, you stole my heart," he replied in his usual cheesy manner. His playful banter was always received by a welcoming twinkle in his wife's eyes.

Inside the police car, Robbie was running his hands over everything with youthful glee. His young mouth dripped with excitement as words such as "cool," "awesome," and "wow" made the moment seem almost festive with his spirit. LJ felt otherwise. He was introduced to how uncomfortable the backseat was. The stiffness of the seat in combination with how it forced your body to hunch over caused a type of psychological suppression within his young mind. The hard plastic against his skin was cold, shocking in a way. Flashes of the black faces he'd seen sitting in the backseat of other police cars scattered within his mind. He would often wonder what they'd done to earn their place in the backseat—a place that seemed destined for all black boys at some point of their lives. It seemed to be a part of the maturation process of becoming a man—an attribute of adolescence.

Now at the age of fifteen, LJ was sitting in the back

of a police car, not as a spectator, but as a potential earner himself. Sweat began to build underneath his knees as he shifted his body to dispel the discomfort. In the backseat, LJ could feel some type of comfort knowing that he wasn't heading to prison, but psychologically, he still felt like a prisoner—a privileged one, nevertheless. While most people in his current position would be cuffed at the wrist, or worse, battered and bruised, he was afforded the luxury of still having some level of control over his body, even if his mind felt otherwise. He had his father to thank for that.

"I just don't understand you boy!" his father said as his hands, which were once fit for boxing, wrapped around the steering wheel. The muscles within his forearms were pulsating as his grip grew tighter. The little vein that was shaped like a lightning bolt was present at his right temple. You could still see some of the discoloration under his right eye from prized fights in his youth.

No words had escaped LJ's lips since they had left the mall. One of the officers recognized LJ after the ruckus and called his dad. The other kids involved weren't so lucky. They were hauled off, heads low, wrists cuffed. As the police cars left the lot, LJ looked on at his friends and the other kids, each eye connecting with his. LJ couldn't do anything but hang his head. Guilt began to crawl atop his shoulders and apply pressure. He'd much rather be with them, in the backseat, facing the same consequences for his involvement. He didn't want the privilege that was afforded to him. He didn't want to be treated differently than his peers. He simply wanted to be one of them. One and the same.

"I keep telling you about hanging with them *damn* boys," his father said through clenched teeth and tight jaws. His jawline was still firm and strong, but you could see some level of softness begin to fill underneath his chin. His eyes were sharp, almost exotic in a way. LJ's mother had always said that he had Egyptian eyes—eyes of a Pharaoh. "You just not going to be satisfied until me or your mother are talking to you through a glass or looking over your body being covered by a white sheet—*are* you?"

LJ sucked his teeth as he looked out of the window. He gazed at the passing faces that looked like his: the old man raising a brown paper bag to his lips, the two men sitting on their front porch in a moment of bellyaching laugher, the lady dancing to the tunes within the confines of her car, the group of kids riding their bikes with hair others deemed to be nappy in search of their next adventure in the night. LJ felt a connection to them. It was a connection that felt rooted. He didn't understand why his father didn't feel that same type of bond. When LJ looked at those faces, he felt they were all one and the same. They weren't "those damn boys." They were people. They were his brothers. Their expectations and dreams were the same as his. Their limitations were the same as his. They were all under the fishbowl of the city. When he was younger, he would stand in the middle of the street and look east, west, north and south and come to the realization that his world, *their* world, was small. There was no pot of gold waiting on the other side of their rainbow, just dark clouds that hung over every head in the city, including his father's. His chances were the same as those of the "damn boys" that were being transitioned to the police station. They were all trapped by the fallacy of life.

Across town, another police car slowly pulled into a parking lot. As they turned off their headlights, one of the officers turned toward the back of the vehicle to the boy who remained quiet the entire ride. He provided no names. He provided no reason. He provided nothing but his physical presence absent his mind.

Bee was lost within his gaze of nightfall as he stared out of the passenger side window. With his arms behind his back, wrists tightly joined together by the steel cuffs and regret falling upon him like a dark cloud, a lone tear broke from his eye. His eyes told him what his heart couldn't. He wasn't exempt from the truth. His fate had already been determined. He was merely a pawn of many on a chessboard.

"What the hell you done got yo'self into?" his father asked as a thick cloud of cigarette smoke fell from his mouth, some curling over his lip. "Did these people fuck with you?" he continued, pointing to the two officers with a dark drunkenness in his eyes.

The policeman proceeded to provide the details of the altercation at the mall. LJ's father had asked the officers to take it easy on Bee. They had agreed and called Bee's father to meet them at the precinct to pick Bee up. They figured that the ride to the precinct would somehow scare him straight. Bee's father leaned against the concrete wall, the powerful glow from the floodlight beaming against the right side of his face, illuminating the long cut across it. "I guess you done did me a favor by not locking his ass up, huh?" His eyes shifted from the officers to Bee. "Locking him up probably would have did his ass some good. The boy is soft... Too soft, if you ask me." One of the officers chuckled as he lifted his hat from his head and placed both hands behind his back. He stared into Bee's eyes who shifted his head down, hiding the truth that were behind them.

"I don't want to see you again—you understand?" the cop said to Bee. Bee nodded his head without making eye contact.

"Do we need to sign some type of papers or something?" his father asked as he smashed the cigarette against the concrete wall, painting a black smudge against it.

"No paperwork. Just keep this kid out of trouble. This could have been a very serious situation where the outcome could have been much different."

"Yeah," his father replied. "Come on, boy. I smell rain coming."

As they walked down the steps, one of the officers shouted, "Hey." Both Bee and his father turned around. "You forgot this," the officer said. Bee extended his hand to grab the black plastic queen chess piece that had fell out of his pocket while he was in the backseat of the police car.

"Thank you," Bee replied with a tenderness in his voice.

As they walked on, his father mumbled to him, "Shid...you almost became a man today, boy." He chuckled before a small laugh fell from his mouth. "Shid...we all got to go in that place at least once in our lifetime. I've been. Your uncles. Your grandfather. Your cousins—hell, your brother shole nuff been. We all done been. Don't let the idea of prison shake you, boy. It's life. So, get used to it." He coughed into one of his hands as he continued, "Why you always carry that queen with you?"

Bee was surprised that his father knew the name of the chess piece that was in his hand.

"That queen is something mighty special, boy. Imagine what it feels like to be the biggest target and threat at the same time. Everybody gunning for ya, but at the same time they fear ya. They know if they can get to ya, then the game be over."

For a moment, Bee heard his grandfather through his father for the first time. He clenched his hand around the chess piece tighter and wondered if his father had ever had a dream.

In his bedroom, LJ tossed a basketball repeatedly toward the ceiling as he lay in bed thinking about what had just happened. He was now on punishment and that meant he'd lost his phone privileges. There would be no calls to Krystal or Bee to check on their well-being. He would simply have to live out the torture through the weekend until he went to school the following Monday. An eerie feeling began to crawl under his skin as his stomach began to churn. The thought of being looked at as a snitch didn't sit well with him. How did the police get there so fast? He hated the fact that his dad was a cop. He became guilty by association. The look in Travis', Ant's and the other boys' eyes told LJ everything he needed to know. He was now an outsider within his own neighborhood and the only thing he was guilty of was trying to be loyal.

"Son…you got a second?" Lorenzo asked as he lightly knocked at the door.

"All I got is time," LJ replied, sarcasm dripping from his tongue.

His father sighed before taking a seat at LJ's desk.

"I know you don't get it now…but in due time you will, son."

LJ kept tossing the ball up, eyes focused on the ceiling.

"I know it's hard for you to understand how certain decisions you make and the people you associate yourself with today can and *will* jeopardize your future."

"They're my *friends*. Friends since kindergarten." LJ shook his head and continued, "I wouldn't expect you to understand."

"What is that supposed to mean?" Lorenzo asked. More bass in his voice.

"Nothing."

"No. It's something. Speak your mind."

LJ continued to toss the basketball toward the ceiling, increasing the pace with more force.

His father stood and caught the ball before it landed back in LJ's hands and said, "Speak your mind." His voice was forceful and demanding. It was a pitch that LJ hadn't grown into yet. A man's voice. Commanding in its way.

LJ's eyes were still fixated on the ceiling, eyebrows furrowed, his breathing rapid. He turned and looked at how his dad towered over him. His father stood six-four and weighed a solid two-hundred and fifty-three pounds. His frame was made for muscles. He had always told his boys that he got his build from working hard as a youth for his father's hauling company: chopping trees, digging holes, chopping wood, gathering wood and hauling bags of dirt over his head for miles in the Mississippi heat. He was big enough physically to be anybody's hero, but to LJ, a hero he was not.

"You don't understand how it is *now*. You're the police. You don't know what's really happening out there. You think everything my friends do is wrong. It wasn't even our fault. We didn't even start it."

"Do you even *know* how it started?"

LJ rolled his eyes.

"Just as I thought."

A mask of pity covered Lorenzo's face. Showing restraint and maturity, with both of his massive hands, he spun the basketball before placing it softly in the cup of his son's hands which were positioned against his chest. He said, "Son, I know you *really* think you understand, but *trust* me—you can't even begin to comprehend what I already know.

As the door closed behind LJ's father, the sound of thunder rumbled outside. The naked sky which had been blanketed with darkness was now accompanied by streaks of lightning. Tomorrow would bring more dark clouds to hover over the heads of the locals who were striving to find that natural path of simply understanding the way of survival.

THE LOW REIGN THEORY

The faces of the presidents from George Washington to George H. W. Bush lined the top of the purple and gold wall that was home to Mr. Peterson's ninth grade classroom. A poster of Christopher Columbus standing triumphant on a ship was displayed above the pencil sharpener with the title CONQUEROR emphasized in bold white letters. The words to the pledge of allegiance hovered over the American flag that was nestled in the corner of the room. There were no faces plastered on the walls that mirrored the skin of the kids who sat in the wooden desks. Those faces were only limited to a chapter within the books that rested underneath their desks or as temporary fixtures on the wall like holiday décor during the month of February, only to be disposed of the following month and locked away in a back file or closet—becoming a distant memory in the minds of the kids. It was a type of marginalized history that only depicted them as slaves with a highlight of the greatness of Dr. Martin Luther King Jr. Unbeknownst to them, this type of psychological conditioning would set the tone of a continued miseducation that led to more chinks in the missing links of their chain of identity.

LJ rested his chin on his arms as the substitute teacher with the monotone voice tried to gain control of the classroom. In addition to the annoyance the tone of his voice was to the ear, the man with the untidy mustache that hid his upper lip spoke slow and stretched his vowels with each word. "Pleeeaaaseee bee quuuiiieeet!" he said in his best attempt at a demand. His message was received by an elevation to the current state of chaos.

One kid wearing a Michael Jordan t-shirt stretched at the collar was talking through one of the box fans doing his best Robocop imitation mouthing a long and robotic, "Fuuuuuuck yooooou," to the substitute. Two girls who had braids draped over their shoulders with colorful beads trapped at the ends with rubber bands and aluminum foil as they played a game of SOS on the back of their assignments. A group of boys was huddled by the lockers playing pencil break, holding the attention of their audience like a headlining boxing match. A substitute teacher was the perfect vacation, second only to seeing a bulky television being wheeled into the classroom.

The morning had been rather quiet about the incident over the weekend. Bee wasn't at school and LJ still hadn't spoken to Krystal. LJ's nonchalant attitude and voluntary solitude had caused some to whisper. They weren't directed toward him, but that would soon come to an end.

A kid sitting in the wooden desk in front of LJ was rubbing his arm due to the sting of being punched by one of his peers for saying a word that began with the letter S. The game was called "Strawberry," and the participants had to say "strawberry" to avoid being punched if a word that began with the letter S escaped their lips. The ones that were able to avoid the pain from being punched by swarming fists usually were the ones that were quick to think. LJ was one of those kids, but he did not participate in the game that day.

Still trying to get over the pain in his right arm, the boy said, "Y'all hear about what happened at Southbrook on Saturday?" The conversation had caught LJ's attention and he began to eavesdrop. Beads of sweat formed atop his head and the queasiness in his stomach that had been settling all morning came back.

"Mane, I heard somebody got shot in the leg."

A boy with a dingy white t-shirt with stains under the pits, stood and began punching the young man doing the talking.

"*Strawberry*—shit!" the boy screamed, only for more punches to come his way. He gathered his bearings and became defensive. "What I say?" His eyes were widened, and anger began to build within. More punches came his way. "Man, anybody else hit me, I'm *fucking* them up," he demanded in his state of confusion.

"Nigga—you ain't fucking nobody up. You said, 'shit' and 'say'—strawberry, strawberry."

"Fuck this game, I quit. As I was *saying*..." His eyes darkened as he looked about, daring someone to punch him. "It was crazy. I heard li'l Travis and 'em got hemmed up by the po-pos." His eyes cut in the direction of LJ as he continued, "LJ...you *was* there—right?" A sneaky smile formed on the boy's face.

LJ maneuvered his head, allowing the left side of his face to rest atop his forearms as he mumbled, "Yeah, I was there."

The small group of boys were now fixated on LJ.

"What happened?" one yelled.

"I heard Freddie was fucking folks up," another added.

"Who fired the shot?" someone asked.

LJ didn't like the way the line of questions was being targeted toward him. He felt as if he was in the back of his dad's police car again.

"Why didn't you get hemmed up with them if you were *with* them?" the boy in the desk in front of him asked.

LJ felt as if all those prying eyes were burning a hole in his skin.

"Why didn't you get hemmed up, LJ?" the boy asked again.

"I'on know," LJ replied, becoming irritated.

"How *you'on* know?" the boy probed. "Travis, Ant, Freddie *and* hell, I heard even li'l Bee got hemmed up—how *you* get out of it?"

The nervousness that had been building within LJ was turning into anger. It was an anger that was hungry for retribution. It was a defiance and a type of retaliation that was reserved only as a means of escape. He knew that no matter how he responded verbally to the question, the truth would be bent and distorted to fit the narrative of the storyteller where a lie could be a truth and a truth could be a lie. For once, LJ decided to take matters into his own hands. LJ reached under his wooden desk. In his hands was a book that was thick and rich with American History—white American History. With a violent swing the book met the face of the boy in front of him. The impact of the blow was loud enough to catch the attention of the entire classroom, something the sub had been unsuccessful at doing. A tussle ensued.

Sitting in the office, the boy holding his face and LJ slouched in his chair, face still scrunched up with anger, they awaited their fates. LJ knew that there would soon be repercussions to his actions. It wasn't the fact the he had retaliated the way he did, but it was *who* he had retaliated against. The boy was a resident of the projects that was only separated from the school by a flimsy wire fence. The kids from those same projects and the kids from the surrounding neighborhoods, which LJ was from, had been engaging in conflict all year. With the end of the year approaching, many understood that there would be plenty of fights along the way. For the most part, LJ had been able to steer clear of the territorial beef, but he now found himself right in the thick of it.

The two boys straightened their postures when Mrs. Williams walked into the office. The boys' eyes followed her as she walked past the oak bookshelf, the memorabilia from Principal Oakley's golden years, the iron file cabinet... She saw sorrow in the boys' faces. Terrance fixed his lips and mouthed, "Mama Wil—"

Mrs. Williams lifted her hand to silence Terrance. Her face was stone—eyes tender, but stern. The pearl bracelet on her arm shifted down slightly. Her perfume followed her like an aura as she positioned herself right in front of the two boys. Mama Williams, as the students called her, is a name that she had earned over the years as the key secretary at the school. There was no lie or mischievous behavior that could escape her reach. The level of respect that she received from the "uncontrollable" or "unruly" youth left many of the staff envious. She didn't have a golden ticket or magical string to their hearts, all she provided was that same level of respect and compassion to their needs that she demanded. She showed them that she cared. She earned her name.

She sighed. "Terrance," she began. "You're just going to continue to make a fool out of me, huh?"

Terrance fixed his mouth to answer again, only to be shushed.

"The last time you were called to Mr. Oakley's office, I saved your butt from being expelled. Do you even want to be in school, boy?" She then diverted her attention toward LJ. "And Mr. Johnson—I must say that this is quite the surprise seeing *you* here."

LJ lowered his head.

"Don't think for one second that I haven't been noticing *your* behavior over the last couple of months. I don't know what it is about the end of junior high school that makes some of y'all act out of character."

Terrance's and LJ's eyes caught each other's for a split second before they shifted them back toward the ground.

"This foolishness is just beneath the *both* of you. The both of you have so much potential, *yet* here we are. I don't even want to know what happened. All I know is, it *stops* right here. Do I make myself clear?"

Terrance clicked his teeth and LJ mumbled a word that Mrs. William's ears didn't catch. "Do I make myself clear?" she repeated.

"Yes ma'am," both boys replied in unison.

"You young people today are just lost, plain and simple, through no fault of your own. You don't know what you don't know, yet you think you know everything." She allowed a chuckle to escape her mouth before she continued, "It's like this generation is simply satisfied with having such a negative mentality. I guess that's why they call it the Low Reign."

The boy's eyes caught each other's again as they tried to decipher what Mrs. William's was trying to say. They were able to find a moment to bond in the midst of the scolding.

LJ raised his hand. "I don't even know what that mean."

"It *means* that this generation—you know what, let me stop just marginalizing it to *your* generation, because the ocean is much deeper than that." She placed her hands in her lap as her fingers locked and continued, "Low reign basically means that at times *we,* as *in all of us"*—she rubbed the dark side of her skin for emphasis—"*we* tend to shoot for the stars instead of the moon. Meaning we set our level of expectations so low that we get satisfied by just simply being. We accept things as they are as opposed to how they *could* or *should* be. We believe what others say about us on the television, even in these very classrooms in some instances, but you know Momma Williams will always tell it straight. Young, beautiful, black boys, I just want you to know that your life is worth more than *that* and you deserve the moon and nothing less than that. So I want you to act like it. *Stop* this foolishness already."

The two boys sat in silence as the weight of guilt from the words of Momma Williams caused them to drop their heads, only to raise them back up by the gentle touch of her hands against their chins.

The sloppy laughs and erratic outburst created a scene Bee had only seen on the television screen. The ambiance shaped by the soul music playing in the background had one man standing on his feet, eyes closed, liquor seeping from his pores, shuffling and allowing his limbs to bend and twist in such a way that was reserved for only those born with rhythm.

"This right here is Two-Can Sam. We call him Two-Can—well, it's kind of self-explanatory," Bee's father said as one of those drunken sloppy laughs fell from his mouth. Two-Can tilted his hat, which was leaning heavy toward the right side of his head, at the young man standing before him. The toothpick hanging from his mouth moved with precision against his lips as he sang the words, "They call me Two-Can Sa-a-am, cause I ain't worth a da-a-amn." He slapped his leg then the back of Bee's shoulder as he proceeded to have one of those belly-aching laughs that old drunks tended to have.

Bee nodded and extended his hand to the man drinking from two beers. "Nice to meet you," he mumbled, avoiding eye contact.

"You got you a respectable boy here, ol' Charlie Chess—respectable boy." He focused his attention to Bee and continued, "Don't pay us no mind. We mean no harm. We just like to jive a little. We just all old friends who like to talk about the good ol' days and just be men for a change. I can tell ya straight…it's hard for a man to be a man these days."

Bee's eyes scoured the old run-down venue. A large aluminum tube could be seen hanging from the empty space in the ceiling. A juke box covered in dust was located by the entrance. It had a dust-free streak across the front, probably by the hands of someone with old eyes not being able to read the list of songs. A man with skin darker than Bee's managed the bar area. He hadn't let a smile crack the straight look of his face, only a giggle here and there. Sitting opposite Two-Can Sam was a man whose head hung low as if it would snap from his neck at any time. Bee always heard his grandfather say that life had a way of weighing heavy on a man's mind, but Bee had never seen it literally until then, unless it was just the liquor. Bee wondered what the man meant when he said that they were just "being men for a change." Did their manhood disappear when the light hit them, like a vampire? Was manhood something that could only hide in the space of an old juke joint like the one he was sitting in? And why was he calling his father Charlie Chess? He soon learned that there was more to his father than he'd known.

Charles woke up that morning before the sun broke, shaking Bee's ankles at the foot of his bed. As Bee mumbled a groggy word or two from underneath his covers, Charles said, "You can sleep in today. No need to rise and shine. You not going to school today. You comin' with me." Those words hit Bee like a beam of light in the morning. As he sat moon-eyed in bed, he wondered what would become of the day. He didn't mind missing school, but he also didn't look forward to spending more time with Charles.

Inside the venue, Charles stood near a pole, legs crossed at the ankles, talking to one of the few lady patrons in the hole-in-the-wall venue. Her legs were long, hips round, buttocks protruding. Charles patted his handkerchief over his forehead as he began to whisper words that Bee was certain his mother wouldn't approve of. He guessed his father was just being a man. He waved for Bee to come toward him.

"It's some more people I want you to meet," he said. His breath was heavy with tobacco and a hint of peppermint.

They walked through a door that seemed like a detour to a forbidden room. Bee got a glimpse of what happened behind the scenes at a restaurant/bar. He watched how the cooks, sweat dripping from their heads, cooked their eggs, steak and toast at the same time on a long, stainless steel stove that looked nothing like his mom's. They walked past the mousetrap that was hiding between the hot water heater and the small hole in the deep corner of the kitchen. They walked into the cooler where there was a mountain of boxes and two men standing at a distance that seemed too invasive to Bee, looking as if they were talking grown-man business. They were too business-like in their appearance to be talking that foolery the old drunks in the front were talking. Bee wanted to bend his ear in on their conversation, but he walked on. To the left of the cooler was another door that Charles knocked on three times in a rhythmic manner. A man with a deep voice asked, "Who is it?"

Charles replied, "Your friendly neighborhood Spider-Man nigguah." He looked back at Bee with a wide smile spread across his face. Catching eyes, Bee looked on at the man whom he couldn't remember the last time he called dad. His hair was even all the way around, deep with waves. "Good hair" is what his mom used to say, effortless. His skin was dark like Bee's. His dimples sank into his skin, accentuating his smile. His eyes seemed to be a permanent red of late. Bee couldn't remember the last time he'd seen the whites of his eyes.

A man opened the door and they walked in. A cloud of smoke hit Bee like a light wind. A man older than Charles appeared through the cloud. As more smoke fell from his mouth, he stood. He was a rather tall man, looked like he was no shorter than six-four. His slacks were pressed, and he wore a white tank top under a beige linen short-sleeved button-down shirt. A brimmed hat rested on his head. One of his front teeth was trimmed in gold. Capturing Bee's attention, he said, "So this here is your boy, huh Charlie?"

Charles nodded.

"Your old man tells me that you good at this game called chess."

The old man now had Bee's full attention.

"I heard you even beat ol' Shifty-Eyes too. Your granddad told me a lot about you boy."

Bee searched his father's eyes for more information as to who this man standing before him was.

"Don't look at your father. I's the one talking to ya. Ya always look a man in the eyes when they talkin' to ya. Specially 'round this way. Ya gotta watch how a man move and how his hands jitter…eyes shift. Ya never know what be going on in a man's head."

Bee focused his attention back on the man.

"Well—let's see what ya got."

Bee walked closer and through the smoke, his eyes focused in on a chessboard that had been already set up. As he sat, he turned his head to look at Charles. For the first time in a long time he allowed a smile to mask his face due to something Charles had done for him and the smile was returned by his dad.

BEE'S HONEY

Nectar. The drink of the gods. The sweet secret a flower holds within its heart. A treasure of bees. As Charles dipped his biscuit in the thick golden honey slathered across his plate, he smiled, remembering how his son, Bee, used to eat the sweet treat straight out of the jar, often leaving a sticky trail from the kitchen floor to the sink. As he grazed the edge of his plate with his finger, catching all the honey and biscuit remnants, with a mouth that was half-full he said, "That old man was kind of rough on you today, huh?"

Charles wanted to continue to treat Bee. So, he took him to one of his favorite restaurants. Bee, removing the crust from his last piece of toast, stacking it atop the others, replied as he hunched his shoulders, "I guess so."

Charles laughed lightly as if he'd heard a private joke. Dimples exposed. "Listen man—I knew you didn't want to hang out with me today, but you got to admit, even if it was just for a split second—you had a good time, *right*?"

Playing a game of chess against someone other than himself was indeed a treasure for Bee. Even though the old man was able to "checkmate" Bee, he had gained so much in return. He didn't realize it at the time, but he had been playing a game within a game. When Bee had first walked into the establishment, he was immediately apprehensive of the faces that crowed the venue. He'd figured them to be nothing more than mirrors of Charles: simple drunks. However, the more time he spent with them, the more he began to understand their manhood and what it represented. He'd learned that those men had more layers to them. It was those additional layers of hurt, insecurity, protection, ego, pride, depression and self-esteem that made them the perfect imperfections of themselves. They were men, not simple drunks. There is nothing simple about manhood, or humanity for that matter. In human form, we're all just complicated beings trying to make sense of the world in which we live. As a black man, the complexities of manhood were even more challenging. In that rundown venue were men who once had dreams of their own, but life had had its way with them, causing them to defer those dreams. There were men who had wives at home, but still entertained the company of other women. It was the same appetite for women that had been passed down by the generations before them. There were men who guarded painful secrets. There were men who were free to tap back into their boyhood, which was still living inside of them. It allowed their youthful spirit to spill over into a couple of *muthafuckas* and those belly-aching laughs. There was a complexity to manhood and humanity that Bee had yet to understand. Bee had learned that those laughs were simply masks. Masks that, if only for a second, allowed them to escape whatever hard-knock life that was awaiting them when they walked out those doors and went home. Bee knew about the demons that followed Charles home. He wondered what type of demons followed the others. Did they creep up in the night and in the early morning? Through it all, Bee did have a good time. In his time at The Shack, Bee had allowed himself to just *be* after a weekend that had left him at odds about who he was and where was he going.

"I guess you can say that," Bee replied.

Charles nodded. "You know uhm—" Charles cleared his throat as he began to choke on the words of affection that were clouded within his mind. "—You know I mean well." He paused, searching his son's eyes, hoping he wouldn't have to say what he was feeling. Charles had been raised on the understanding that men didn't bond with a type of tenderness which expressed an emotion that should have been natural: love. His love had been boiled down to gestures such as a head nod, sharing a laugh or the quick pound of a fist. Words such as, "I love you boy" were usually said with a touch of aggression so as not to be confused with a layer of softness. However, as a father, he knew Bee needed more; he just didn't know how to provide it.

"Can I ask you a question?" Bee asked.

"What is it?"

"Did you ever have a dream—like when you was my age?"

Charles leaned back against the hard plastic of the booth inside the restaurant and exhaled deeply as if a bad memory had been resurrected. He rubbed his hands over his head, causing deep lines to form at the center of his forehead. It was a question he didn't expect from Bee. It was a question he hadn't thought about in years. What was a dream to a man—a black man in the United States of America? Charles said the first logical thing that made sense to him. "I mean *sure*—everybody got a dream."

"What was yours?"

"Times were different when I was yo' age. When I was yo' age it was around sixty-five or sixty-six. Different times kid. At that time my dream was to simply get out of poverty." His eyes darkened as he continued, "You know, me and my old man didn't see eye-to-eye much. He wanted *more* from me. *More* than I was willing to give at the time. I took a different path. My journey was *tight* and narrow. So, I really didn't dream much. Hell, I couldn't afford too. My shit had to be real."

"You didn't ever, like, think about being more than, like, a regular person. Like a star or something?"

He laughed. "Naw kid. By the time I was yo' age, I was a full-grown man, playing a full-grown man's game in a world that was teaching me that I didn't belong. At least I thought I was anyway." He paused. "Now when I was *really* younger, like maybe five or something, I wanted to be a weatherman."

Bee laughed.

"What's so funny?" Charles returned the laugh. "*Yeah*...I wanted to be a weatherman. I wanted to predict the rain and shit. I used to sit outside and wait for Pops to get home. I used to be like, 'Dad, I bet I know when the rain coming. I can smell it.' He'd look at me all twisted up about the face and say some shit like, 'Boy, you'on know shit 'bout no weather.'" Charles' eyes ventured off into space as if he was facing his dad again. He shook his head. "Then I learned really quick how much of a *dream* that was. My nigga ass couldn't be no weatherman. Then I started to think more about reality. You see—your grandad didn't treat me like he treated you. He was so busy putting food on the table and keeping a roof over our heads that we didn't talk very much. Looking back, I guess he did his job as a man and provided for us."

Charles studied Bee's face some more and asked, "Now let me ask *you* a question." Concentrating on his eyes, he asked, "Sex? You ever had some honey boy?"

Bee lowered his eyes and dropped his head.

Charles maneuvered his head in an attempt at catching Bee's eyes again. "I mean—you *are* into girls, right?" he asked as he let out a chuckle.

Bee lifted his head and fixed his face in a manner as if Charles had asked him a stupid question. Absurd even. Of course, he liked girls. Bee nodded and said, "I ain't done it yet, *but—*"

"*But* nothing." Charles replied. "Shiiid. I was probably two years older than you are now when yo' brother

Junior was born. And befo' then—shiiid—I was knocking them down like bowling pins. But when Junior was born—" His eyes cast sadness as he leaned back. Deep exhale.

Bee fell silent.

"You *know*—you know you got a good heart on you," Charles said abruptly, changing the subject.

When Charles wasn't drunk or high, he spoke with clarity. There seemed to be some type of sense about his words. They weren't just a bunch of rambling nothings.

"There's a curse about having a good heart though, boy." He shifted in his seat as he continued, "When you got a good heart, people tend to take *it* and you for granted. They try to get over on you. Hell…sometimes you may take *yourself* for granted. You do stuff you really don't want to do…all on account of having a good heart. People like to play on emotions. Hell, even the church do it at times. Guilt you into things, like the whole thing about heaven and hell."

"Is that a bad thing?" Bee asked.

"I'm not saying if it's bad or good. I'm just saying you got to guard that. Be protective of it."

"Do you got a good heart?"

"My heart done turned cold a long time ago, kid."

Bee fell silent again.

"Listen…I know things between me and yo' momma ain't been the best lately. I hate you got to see some of that shit, but it's some shit about being a man you just can't understand yet. Sometimes yo' momma don't allow me to be a man when I need to be."

Bee wanted to ask him more about Charles' and his mother's relationship. He wanted to ask why he had to put his hands on her. Why did he have to berate her? Is that what being a man represented? Exuding your physical and mental dominance? However, he fell silent again as he hadn't developed into his manhood enough to be bold enough to ask such a question. But there was no doubt that he'd grown that day. And one day that conversation would be had. He would be bold enough to tell Charles how close he'd been to going in the kitchen to grab a knife and stab him in the chest while he slept on the couch hungover. He'd tell him how he'd found his gun under the mattress and had visions of loading it with the bullets that he kept hidden behind the lamp on his side of the bed, to take one to two shots to Charles' chest if he had put his hands on Bee's mother again. He'd tell him about the nights when he allowed his tears to soil his pillows, wishing that Charles would die or get put away in jail never to return. He would tell him why he'd never called him 'dad' and ask why he'd never called him 'son.' He'd ask why Charles never attended any of his school functions or took interest in any of his boyhood adventures. He'd ask why. One day he would, but on the day when he sat across from Charles and saw the vulnerability in his eyes for the first time, he just enjoyed it. Looking back into his eyes, he fixed his mouth and asked, "Dad…why you never told me you played chess?"

The weather was ripe for play. Birds flocked to the trees that had birthed the best fruit. Marching ants built their forts from the residue of the recent storm. Driveways and sidewalks were decorated with various colors of chalk as girls hopped from square to square. Sugar-filled drinks dripped from the mouths of young faces as cookie crumbs became glued at the corners. Clouds of dirt took form as boys, with sweat dripping from their brown skin, bounced balls and leaped into their imaginations as the next basketball superstar. The wheels of bicycles spun as the soda cans that were wedged between the seat and back wheels mimicked the sound of a roaring engine. Kids flipped, contorted, and tossed their bodies from hills, rivaling the moves of a professional gymnast. The weather was ripe for play and the youth reaped the sweet benefits of it.

LJ waved his hands and danced away from the bumblebee that was aroused by the sweet scent he'd sprayed across his chest. He stumbled against one of the bricks that his mother had told him to haul into the backyard before she came home. "Shit," he said as he looked down at his sneakers, a deep scuff mark now scraped across it. He dusted himself off from the fall, wiping away the loose grass and mulch from his clothing and from his head. He noticed a rush of kids running his way. They were pointing. Laughing ad nauseam. "Y'all go on back to playing ball. Don't come over here with that shit." He stared the young boys down.

His little brother Robbie was tossing the football to himself. "Can you be our all-time quarterback?" he asked LJ. LJ, still trying to remove the scuff marks from his sneakers, shook his head. "Naw man, I don't feel like it today."

One of the other boys approached LJ. He pulled a rag from his back pocket. "Here—use this."

LJ grabbed the rag from the boy and replied, "Yo Malcolm…why you be always writing in that pad? You writing raps or something?"

The young boy's face was handsome. Hair cut low, even all around. "Naw—no raps. I just like to write."

"Yo, we got some more people coming to play ball," a light-skinned boy with green eyes said.

As the newcomers rode their bikes into the driveway, all the other kids began picking the players they wanted on their team.

"I got Chris," one yelled.

"I got BJ," yelled another.

"What's up, LJ?" one of the kids said. He was dressed too clean to be playing football. Roped around his neck was a thin gold chain with a basketball medallion hanging from it. He had on some blue and white Nikes that matched his clothing. The youthful fat still clung to his bones as the coils of his hair sprouted high, faded all around. The boy's name was Mario.

"What's up, Mario? I like those sneaks, yo. Those junts fresh. Where ya boys Pat, Lamar and Tim at?"

"Pat on punishment. Lamar not at home yet. He should be home soon though. Tim down the street playing basketball."

"Come on LJ, can you *please* be the all-time quarterback?" Robbie asked almost begging.

"Aite, but only if y'all play sideline pop. I ain't with that touch football shit."

Robbie smiled as he ran back to tell his group of friends that they now had a quarterback and the game would begin as soon as they decided on their respective teams.

Across the street, a young girl whose complexion was on the lighter side of the brown spectrum stared at the group of boys as they tossed the football to one other. She listened on as adult words slipped from their boyish lips, catching the ears and eyes of the nosy neighbors that peeked through curtains. She was new to the neighborhood and Robbie had been trying to impress her ever since she'd moved in across the street.

Robbie, noticing that she was outside, began to throw the ball as high as he could in the air, only for it to fall gently back into his hands—so he imagined. However, the ball slipped right through the cup of his hands encouraging the slaughter of laughs and phrases such as "nigga you can't catch" or "butter-fingers." Robbie, face red with embarrassment, turned to see if the girl had witnessed his butterfingers in action. She had. She even cracked a smile. Her name was Toya.

"Car time!" a kid yelled, and the kids parted the street like the red sea, allowing the red sedan to pass them. It pulled in front of LJ's house. Stepping out of it was a rather tall boy. He opened the trunk and pulled out a basketball and a pair of shoes. With long strides, he bounced the ball with ease as if it was a part of his natural walk.

"Yo. What up, Chill Will?" LJ yelled.

The boy sat on the curb and placed his sneakers on his feet. He too had a high-top that was faded, with three distinct lines on the side of his head.

Now standing over Will with the football in hand, LJ asked, "What you doing this way?"

"Got a game over at the church at six. You should fall through."

"Is it go be some honeys there?"

Will looked up toward LJ and twisted his mouth. "You know it ain't go be no honeys there—hoopers only."

With a disappointment in his eyes, LJ replied, "Mane—I'm on punishment. I can't even leave the house."

"What happened?"

LJ hunched his shoulders. "It ain't about nothing. Regular Memphis shit."

Will nodded and didn't probe further.

"Yo—I heard a coach from college came to your crib the other day."

"Yeah, it was the weekend before last."

"Who was it?"

"Some school from Georgia."

"Shit…you almost big time."

"You could do the same if you wanted to."

"Mane, they don't be paying me no attention."

"You gotta stay at it. No work. No play. You know the deal."

"LJ come on! We ready to play!" Robbie yelled.

"You gonna chill for a sec?" LJ asked

"Yeah," Will said, stretching. "I'll chill and watch y'all."

Midway through the game, fatigue caught up with the excitement of play. Boys were hunched over, hands to knees, trying to catch their breath. A couple of boys had their heads turned awkwardly as they sucked from the water hose. Cuts and bruises that would last a lifetime and become the foundation for a "remember when" story were present at their elbows. It was the '*hood* halftime.

The light-skinned boy with the green eyes, Chris, walked toward Toya's driveway and said, "Yo, you wanna be our cheerleader?"

She stared down the boy with a sassiness she must have learned from her mother. "Why I gotta be a cheerleader? Why can't I just play?"

"Girls don't play no football."

"Says who?"

Chris waved her off with his hand as Malcolm approached the driveway, his notepad in hand.

"Robbie, you gonna let Malcolm steal your girl?" LJ whispered to Robbie as he placed the bandage on his arm. Robbie looked out and saw that Malcolm was sharing something on his notepad with the girl across the street. She was smiling. Jealousy was on Robbie's face. Malcolm and Toya. The thought burned in Robbie's chest.

"Car time!" one of the kids yelled.

A car drove pass slowly as the kids looked on. Another car was coming up the hill not too far behind. As it approached, the window rolled down and someone yelled, "SNITCHING ASS NIGGA! POLICE ASS NIGGA!"

Will stood and caught eyes with LJ.

"What was that about?" Will asked, eyes widened with curiosity.

"Memphis shit," LJ replied.

Some faces held confusion as others continued as if it was all normal. LJ stuffed his hands deep in his pockets as the same guilty feeling rose within his chest. A bee flew past his ear, and he caught the sound. It landed in his mother's flowerbed in search of something sweet. It was searching for the sweet nectar. LJ was searching for something he did not know. Summer was approaching and he knew that there would be more Memphis shit waiting in the wings. His honey wasn't sweet. He was in the Low Reign.

GOD'S FED UP

Music. It's the melodic tones that pull at the ear bringing one down to life's rhythm. Music is where memories resonate. Music is life in raw form. It's a twitch of emotions that makes one either drown in their emotions from their spirit of choice or swim in a current of joy and happiness. Music is life and it was alive and well in the Low Reign.

A swirl of smoke was broken by a large hand as it fanned away the evidence. Kids were walking by. A man with one hand behind his back, hiding the joint that was burning into a roach, told the kids to move along and get away from the grown folks' business. Al Green was entertaining the group of family, friends and neighbors who were celebrating the beginning of the summer of 1991.

Lorenzo drew his face away from the black grill as a thick cloud of smoke covered his face. The scent was of hickory and sweet pine. Inside the grill was a slab of ribs, smoked sausages and bologna. The smoked sausages had multiple slits along their bellies, and they were slightly burnt to perfection as the meat broke away from the red skin. The bologna was thick, cut to the center and mopped with a sweet homemade sauce. It, too, was slightly burnt to perfection. Lorenzo wiped his eyes which burned from the intense smoke. He grabbed his light beer, his choice for controlling his weight, and called for his wife Betty.

The sun had been blinding all day. Betty glanced toward the naked area where her oak tree used to reside. On days such as this, she would get angry at Lorenzo again for cutting it down, only to replace it with a dog pit that had never been used. Before long, the sun would be setting, but the stubborn heat would remain.

Betty was sitting at the wrought iron table with cards in hand, swaying her head from side to side as she sipped on the fruity drink that Ms. Debbie, the neighbor across the street, had brought over. Betty's brother, Uncle Buck, was grinning across the table. He took his last pull of the joint before setting the roach inside the empty beer can. "Pass me another one of nem drinks," he shouted. Pop, soda or cola wasn't in the repertoire of the Memphis locals. A drink was simply called a drink…no matter the type.

Uncle Buck stood up abruptly. "Ohhh Shit. That's my *jam*," he shouted as Curtis Mayfield's "Diamond in the Back" broke up their game of spades.

"Sit yo' ass down and play the card Buck…*damn*," his wife Kat retorted. She was always glamorous in her appearance. Puffy curls sat atop her head, and her eyes popped with color. Her wrist jingled as she moved her hands to pull Buck back down to his seat. Puma, Betty's youngest brother, sat across from Betty at the table. He took a swig of his drink as he swatted away a pesky mosquito.

"This song is about life," Buck said. He was high on the music and marijuana. "Tell 'em Curtis… Be thankful *got damned* for what you got." He rocked his hips to the riffs of the guitar as he yelled, "BE THANKFUL muthafuckas." Kat shook her head when Buck finally made his way back into his seat.

Robbie, wearing a He-Man t-shirt stained with grass and juice, approached the table.

"What you need, baby?" Betty asked Robbie.

"What time the food gone be ready?"

"It won't be too much longer. Where is your brother?"

"Uhm. He still in his room with his girlfriend."

"That boy betta not be up in that room with that girl," Betty said as she rose to her feet.

"Let that boy enjoy hisself, Betty, *damn*," Buck said.

"He can enjoy *himself* right out here—with the rest of us."

Betty, finally hearing her husband call for her over the music, lifted her finger as she headed toward the front.

"Aye boy," Buck called to Robbie. "Bring ya uncle one of nem drinks over there. Ain't nobody brought me shit yet."

"Give me a dolla," Robbie challenged.

"I'll give you a ass whoopin'. How 'bout dat? And somebody go help Lorenzo with that damn meat. All the shit go be burnt soon enough."

LJ's wiry body rested firm against the wall of his room with his legs pulled up to his chest. Krystal sat close, nestled against his body: legs stretched, skirt slightly raised over her knees. She fidgeted with her nails as LJ bobbed his head to the sounds of "Endangered Species" from Ice Cube's *Amerikkka's Most*

Wanted tape.

"You never answered me," Krystal said, breaking the silence.

LJ raised a brow and replied, "Answered you about what?"

Krystal stood. With one of her hands she flicked her hair from her shoulder to her back. "Like my braids?"

LJ no longer bobbed his head to the music. He was eye level to her thighs. He pulled his bottom lip in as he stared. His heart accelerated. LJ envisioned her standing there with no skirt to hide the secret levels of her upper thighs.

She nudged him with her bare feet, toes painted, glittered at the top. "Do you like them or *what*?"

He tilted his head toward her face and replied, "Yeah…but I like something else even more."

She placed her hand over her mouth as she smiled to hide her braces. "Why you always playing?"

LJ stood. Krystal now had to tilt her head toward his. "Who said I'm playing?" LJ asked. She stared down the boy whose hormones showed in his eyes. She looked on at how his shirt clung tight enough for her to see a glimpse of the cut of his chest. When she'd first touched his chest months ago, she had been aroused at how tight and firm it was. She, too, wondered what it would be like to see him bare.

LJ pulled her close to steal a kiss. She didn't reject. It was quick. A peck. LJ pulled back. Krystal, still looking into his eyes, pulled him back in. She, too, stole a kiss, longer than the last. Youthful smiles spread their faces. Neither knew what to say or do next. Shyness masked their faces. Inexperience was cutting through their blissful fabric.

"You want to sit on the bed?" LJ asked as he reached for her hand.

Krystal, holding his hand, led him toward the bed. No words. Their hearts were beating frantically. Butterflies in their stomachs. Nerves jittery.

Sitting on the edge of the bed, Krystal kicked at her shoes on the floor as she rolled her thumbs in circles. LJ's eyes scoured the room as his face turned hot. He exhaled and stretched one of his arms across her shoulders. Ice Cube's "Who's the Mack?" was now playing in the background. LJ tried his best to be one, but a Mack he wasn't.

LJ sensed that Krystal was tense. She shied her eyes away from his as she stared down at her skirt, thumbs still twirling away. LJ allowed his hand to stroke her hair, causing the beads on the ends to sound off in clicks and clacks.

"I can get use to this," he said.

"To what?"

"This. You. Us."

LJ pulled her closer to him. She exhaled as she raised her legs off the ground in a nervous heap. Her hands laid limp at her sides, one on his sheets and the other close to his leg. LJ leaned in for another kiss. Another peck. Their eyes met. They both leaned in again. LJ inadvertently grazed her breast with his hand. They stopped. Nervous eyes, faces hot. Beads of sweat formed against their foreheads. The door opened. Betty entered the room to break up the friskiness of their teenage love affair.

"*Uhm*—why are y'all up here? And what the hell are you listening to LJ?"

The experience of the inexperienced was over.

"I *hope* y'all not up here trying to be grown. Boy, you still color in coloring books."

Krystal snickered.

LJ hung his head and hid his eyes as he dragged his feet toward the door.

In the living room, some of LJ's younger cousins were dancing on the oriental rug that the coffee table usually sat upon. The table was now placed in the corner of the room, setting the stage for the ultimate dance floor. One of his cousins, a boy with a slim frame and curl atop his head was flailing his arms back and forth, one after the other, as he bent his knees and twisted his body and shouted, "Do the Humpty-Hump, come on and do the Humpty-Hump."

Betty was in the kitchen tilting a bag of sugar over a pitcher of red and purple Kool-Aid. Puma was leaning on her shoulder begging to get the keys to her car.

"LJ, you want to tell your uncle what you were up there doing?" Betty said.

Puma stared down the juvenile who often reminded him of himself. Even though LJ was growing into the spitting image of his father, he still had subtle features of his mom and Puma.

Smiling at LJ and Krystal, Puma asked, "What she talkin' 'bout nephew?"

Krystal's eyes were still at her feet. LJ rolled his eyes. "Wasn't nobody doing nothing. Just listening to the radio. That's all."

Puma read through the bullshit in his lie. He poured a cup of the Kool-Aid.

"Sweet enough?" Betty asked. She then stared down the girl who had just been sitting on the edge of a bed with her first-born son. She pitied the girl. "No need to be shy now, honey. Come on over here and fix you a plate." She looked at LJ, "Better yet...LJ, *you* come make her a plate. Since you wanna be grown and all."

"I'm not hungry, ma'am."

Betty stared her down and replied with a "Uhm...hmm, LJ make her a plate anyway. She can take it with her."

"Yes ma'am."

"Thank you, Mrs. Johnson."

"Uhm hmm."

Puma was still following behind her when she said, "Puma—no. You not getting my car to go see no girl. I see where that nephew of yours is getting this foolishness from."

Outside, Lorenzo had just closed the lid to the grill as he had pulled the last of the smoked sausages from it. He nibbled on Betty's ear as he handed the plate of pork to her. Everyone enjoyed watching the two love on each other.

"I'm telling y'all, Jack Kevorkian is a crazy muthafucka!" Buck said.

"Who said he wasn't?" Kat replied.

"Evidently you muthafuckas did…as y'all don't see nothing wrong with what he did."

"Awl…cut the bullshit Buck and deal the damn cards."

"And another thing—I'm tired of muthafuckas always talking about the crime in the black communities as if those white people out east ain't got they own damn problems," Buck added.

"Now you talkin' some sense Lorenzo added.

Lorenzo and Betty were curled into each other's arms. They both nibbled on a piece of rib together, sharing subtle bites to the bone from each other's hands.

"You need to talk to that son of yours," Betty whispered as Bobby Womack played in the background.

She wiped her hands, freeing them from the barbeque residue.

"I'm the last person that boy wants to talk to about now."

She chuckled. "Sometimes I just wish I could shrink him back to being my baby boy."

Lorenzo sighed. "He's just smelling himself a little. We all went through the phase."

"I know. I guess I'm just not ready for him to grow up, that's all."

Lorenzo rubbed one of her arms as he replied, "Come on now, that's the beauty of being a parent. Get them to the point of being responsible enough to take care of themselves." He leaned in close enough for his breath to heat her neck as he continued, "Besides, the sooner they get out the house, the sooner we can…" He whispered something in her ear that made her insides tingle.

"Officer Johnson you better watch it, I may do something that will make you pull out that gun of yours."

They both snickered as if *they* were the mischievous teens sneaking love words and touches to each other.

"God must be fed up with our asses the way he got this got damn heat going," Uncle Buck shouted from across the yard.

"That brother of your is something else," Lorenzo whispered.

"Something else indeed," she replied with a smile across her face.

LJ walked outside with a face towel draped over his shoulder. In his peripheral was his little brother Robbie and a friend trying to catch lightning bugs in a jar. His little cousin was blowing and chasing bubbles against the late day. Some of the neighborhood kids were sliding their bodies across the blue slip-n-slide in the grass, welting their bellies with each slide. Kids whose lips were sticky from popsicles played hand games as they lied about their upcoming summer adventures.

Opening the gate to the backyard, LJ walked in.

"Ma…I'm about to walk Krystal home."

Waving her hand at Krystal, she replied, "Y'all be safe. Did you get that plate?"

LJ held the paper plate covered with aluminum foil in the air.

His mother nodded.

"Nephew. How the hell did the Lakers lose to the Bulls?

LJ hunched his shoulders as he turned to walk back out the gate. LJ had cried when Michael Jordan and the Bulls had defeated Magic Johnson and his Lakers, making it Jordan's first NBA championship.

LJ soon heard his Uncle Buck and Aunt Kat getting into a heated argument. Alcohol tended to induce loose lips, share secrets and make words cut deeper in the Low Reign. LJ knew that he was leaving at the right time.

As LJ and Krystal neared the block to her street, they stopped at the corner. The sounds of night and the streetlights surrounded them. LJ looked up at the gnats and mosquitos chasing the streetlight.

"See you *tomorrow*?" LJ asked.

Swinging their arms while holding hands, Krystal replied, "Can't."

"Why not?"

"I gotta go over to my grandma's house for a week."

"Damn. What am I supposed to do for a week?"

She laughed. "You can *call* me, ya know."

"Mom's be trippin' sometimes about that phone."

"I understand," she whispered, disappointed that their night was about to come to an end. She then saw the light to her front porch turn on and soon the opening of the front door followed. A high-pitched voice yelled, "Kryyyystal."

"I gotta go," Krystal said in a rush.

They hugged. No kiss—got to be discreet.

"I'll call you tonight," she said.

LJ nodded and watched her walk to the house. Inside was a feeling he'd never known: love.

On the way home, LJ was stopped by some of Robbie's friends: Malcolm, Chris and BJ. They were at the edge of a driveway playing with a cigarette lighter.

"What y'all little bad asses doing?" LJ asked.

"Minding our business," BJ, the short stocky one, replied.

LJ shook his head and laughed.

LJ's smile soon turned to concern as he noticed a

figure hunched over, back to a tree. His shirt was stretched long at the collar. Splashes of blood were caked on the boy's shirt. As LJ approached, he noticed that the boy's lip was busted, and a long cut was across his face.

The boy was Bee.

When morning broke, the air was already heavy against the locals' necks. The sun was unrelenting, searing the concrete that housed the colorful creativity of the kids the day before. The mugginess was disrespectful like a mouthy child to an adult. Even the birds chirped their complaints as they sat upon branches, blanketed by the shade of the tree.

Bee rested his naked skin against the hood of his mother's car which sat under the carport. His hair was freshly cut, face oiled, skin glistening from the petroleum jelly he used to fight any potential ash. He even had a healthy portion of deodorant under his arms. He grabbed the shirt that was draped over his shoulder and wiped his forehead with it before tossing it into the corner by a collection of empty two-liter soda bottles. Anger was brewing on his insides, but sadness was in his eyes. He'd been waiting for his dad to pick him up since before the sun became untucked by the blanket of night.

Bee's father had told him the night before that he'd take him on another man trip. Even though his words fell from a mouth that was alive with alcohol, Bee had built a trust in the man again. He believed his words. He believed in him.

"I knew I shouldn't have trusted him," Bee said as he wiped an eye that was building up for a tear to fall. "He's probably somewhere too drunk to know where he is," Bee said to himself.

The truth was, his father was sober and cognizant of his whereabouts. He'd wanted to surprise his boy with a gift that would allow his son to flash that smile he'd had when he was playing chess. His father had learned about a chess summer camp that was taking place on the east side of the city. He didn't have the funds for the full tuition, so he spent the better part of the morning filling out job applications. In a supposedly routine traffic violation, he was detained as the police found some drug paraphernalia tucked in the console of his vehicle. It was a package that he had long forgot about, but the past has its way of catching up to you at the most inconvenient time. In his case, it was time with his son. He was now resting his back on a cot inside the Shelby County Jail with disappointment in his eyes.

Bee wished he could have given his dad the benefit of the doubt, but his father's track record wouldn't allow for that to happen.

Bee, now walking up the street shirtless, rubbed his neck as summer's bite was nipping away at his skin. It was quiet. There were hardly any cars coming to or from on the street. The first sound that captured his attention was from a ranch house with green shutters that had a box fan inside one of its windows blowing air into a blue towel that was pressed against it. It reminded him of how his grandmother had once told him about placing a cool towel over a fan to blow in some cool air.

He approached LJ's house. The police car was there. By the back gate, he saw Lorenzo hauling a large bag of charcoal over his shoulder. Bee knew that a spades party was about to happen that evening. Bee wanted to stop to express his anger to his friend, but he decided to walk on.

Bee coughed as he choked on the smoke he'd inhaled. Before leaving his house, he'd stolen a couple of his mom's cigarettes from under the pie dish where she kept all her goodies. Along with the cigarettes, he'd grabbed a couple of food stamps as well. He'd always likened the colorful money to Monopoly funds.

Standing at the corner of Shelby Drive and Neely, Bee blew out a cloud of smoke, not coughing this time, the tickling sensation in his throat was now gone. He crossed the street, the sun highlighting some areas of his back, and he walked into the parking lot to Big Star, the local grocery store. He purchased his essentials: two cakes, a bag of chips and a drink.

When he walked back outside, hand deep into his bag of chips, his eyes bulged to full bloom. He ducked behind one of the drink machines outside, before sneaking off to the area that housed the shopping baskets. With his back against the brick wall, he kneeled as he poked his head around the corner, in view of the blue car with the white top. It was Travis—music loud, bass thumping against the trunk. Bee pulled his head back before he could be seen. More sweat covered his face. He kept taking subtle looks as he bit down on pieces of his cake. He watched as person after person approached Travis' car, extending their hand through the window, only to pull it back and place something inside their pockets.

Bee was concerned because there had been whispers throughout the Low Reign that he and LJ had snitched on Travis and others in exchange for their freedom. And if there was one thing that would land you on Travis' list, snitching was one of them. Bee knew the consequences all too well. One day he would tell Travis what truly happened, but that day wasn't the day as the summer tended to always bring out the worst in people in the Low Reign.

"Can I help you, son?" a man in a white shirt and red tie asked Bee. The man had a light brown balding head and keys clipped to his belt.

"No sir. I was just—" Bee's eyes followed Travis' car as it pulled out of the parking lot and out of distance.

"Well, you can't just hang around back here," the man said.

Bee tossed the cake wrapper in his bag and proceeded to walk away.

"And next time, no shirt, no service. I know you own one, boy."

"Yes sir."

Bee allowed the last remains of his drink to quench his thirst before he tossed the empty bottle into the wooded area from the sidewalk that was decorated with multiple cracks and holes. Behind the overgrown weeds and loose branches, a strong stench usually followed, especially in the summer months. It was believed that a dead body rested underneath all the rubble. At least that's what they'd been told. As Bee quickened his pace, he realized how far he'd walked from home and regretted it as he still had to walk back in the unforgiving heat. He didn't know where to go or what to do next except to keep walking.

It was now well past noon and the city was more alive than it had been. More cars sped by. Bee could hear the chatter and laugher bouncing from yard to yard as he continued his journey to the unknown. The sun had caused his skin to appear a dark-reddish color. As his pants sank lower toward his hips, due to the sweat underneath them, the untanned area showed a clean line. His hair was no longer a shiny soft curl. It was now kinkier and drier, closer to its natural state. The chemicals were washed away by the heat, trickling down his face and neck along with his sweat.

Bee was kicking a soda can along the sidewalk when he heard someone yell toward his direction. Not able to recognize the words, Bee turned toward the voice and the words became clearer.

"Let me holla at you for a second," the voice yelled again.

Bee understood that he was no longer in the comfort of his neighborhood and those words weren't meant to be words of inquiry or endearment. He knew that his knees had better be elevating past his pelvis in a speedy pace soon, if he didn't want to be on the receiving end of an unfortunate event. So, he ran. He ran until his breath could no longer keep up with his legs.

Hunched over, sweat falling from his face, heart pounding against his chest, Bee struggled to catch his breath. An elderly couple stared at the young boy with no shirt panting in front of their yard with apprehension in their eyes.

"What you done did, boy?" the man called out to Bee.

Bee, still panting and heart skipping some beats, struggled to respond.

"You look like you done got yo'self in some shit," the old man yelled. The woman sitting next to the old man nudged him as she placed her glass of iced tea on the round table. She whispered something that agitated the old man before he said, "Come on over here, boy. Come rest ya ass for a minute. Get in some shade."

Bee allowed his eyes to wander every which way before walking through the yard that was well kept compared to the other yards to its left and right.

The old man had on a buttoned-down collar shirt with the sleeves rolled up to his elbows. He had a white towel draped over his shoulder and a blue baseball cap rested on his head. Bee noticed an assortment of moles on the crests of the wrinkles in the old man's skin. His bare feet rested on the concrete.

"Thirsty?" the woman asked.

Bee nodded.

The old woman stood. She reminded him of his grandmother. She was a fair shade of brown with bouncy gray curls atop her head. When she walked inside, Bee looked to the old man. He searched his eyes and when the old man didn't fix his mouth to say anything, Bee dropped his head.

The old man had been studying him as well.

"What you running from?"

Bee shrugged his shoulders.

"*Yeah*...I bet you don't know," the old man replied, sarcasm dripping from his tongue. "*Well*...whatever it is, I hope you've learned a lesson." The old man took the towel that was resting on his shoulder and wiped his forehead before placing it on the table. "What's yo' name boy?"

"Bee," the boy mumbled.

"That's ya real name?"

Bee shook his head. "It's Brandon."

The old man nodded as he sipped his tea. "Where you live?"

"Whitehaven."

"Whitehaven?" the old man asked to confirm. "What the hell you doing all the way 'round this way? You got people over here?"

Bee shook his head.

The old woman returned with an empty Mason jar and something wrapped in a paper towel.

"You just gonna feed the whole damn neighborhood, huh?"

"Glenn, hush already. This boy got hungry written all over his face." She placed the empty Mason jar on the table and handed him the napkin. "Here…it's a tuna sandwich. I got some chips too if you want some."

"Thank you."

It didn't take Bee long to finish the sandwich and iced tea. Bee stood and said thank you again. He looked out into the street as he prepped to face the heat. He figured he'd journey back home, but he'd take another route. Before he turned to leave, the old man stopped him by calling his name. He placed a shiny object into Bee's hand and said, "You take this wit cha and be careful boy." Bee hesitated before placing it in his pocket. "Nellie, gone in there and get this boy a shirt to put on his damned back. If you don't want trouble to follow you, stop looking like it. And pull ya pants up."

Bee's legs were nearly numb as he dragged his feet along the sidewalk. He was almost home, and he had adjusted to the heat. At the corner of Neely and Shelby Drive, Bee felt comfortable to be back on his turf. His surroundings. He was home and Bee dropped his guard. He didn't notice the car that had been following him for the past block until it was too late. As he crossed the street, a car with music deafeningly loud stopped aggressively in front of him. Bee saw two—but it could have been more—people rage toward him. Curled into a ball in the street, Bee withstood an assortment of punches and kicks against his already defeated and withering frame. His mind shifted to the knife that the old man had given to him, but there was no way he could remove his hands from his head. On that street, Bee made a vow to never be the one taking the blows from here on. It was time for him to make his move on the chessboard of life. Like God, Bee was fed up. In Bee's mind all he could think about was the betrayal from a friend—Travis. The next move on the chess board would belong to Bee.

SCRIPTURE ON ICE

The wooden beams holding up the old church nestled in North Memphis were beginning to show their age like bones inside a seasoned body beginning to lose its mass and density. The building was starting to lean in areas where it was once straight and firm. Sitting by the stairs leading up to the building was a bucket, a shovel and a small bag of cement. The front doors, which were now a faded green, had become weakened and hollowed over the years. So much so that one of them was no longer fit to be opened, leaving only one way to enter and exit the church.

Waiting in the vestibule were two senior leaders dressed in white greeting those entering the body of the church. Outdated pamphlets, plastic bags and newspapers were scattered about on the large table that used to hold the current announcements. The walls were still olive in some places, but the discoloration over the years made it look like a dusty yellowish-brown for the most part. On the walls hung pictures of the pastors of the past and images of the building as it aged over the years. Despite its diminishing frame, once you opened the doors to the sanctuary, the inside was still full of spirit like that of a wise elderly person. The heart, which was the congregation, was still beating a strong rhythmic beat.

Inside, LJ shifted his weight from foot to foot as his frame became more restless by the second. With his head still down, he allowed one of his eyes to open. He slightly turned to allow his now roaming eye to scour the small church. The woman standing at the podium had long since provided the announcements, but she was in her routinely extended prayer over the congregation. He witnessed some of the congregation aggressively waving paper fans over their faces with bowed heads and closed eyes. Some wiped the sweat from their necks with cloths. The stale stench of the church often reminded him of the homes of old people. LJ continued to look on as he saw the restlessness in some of the other youths' faces. They stole smiles, sniggers and silly faces from each other. Some of the guardians sensed the disrespect and provided taps against the backs of their heads or stern looks that often led to one closing their eyes and joining in on the prayer—praying that a belt against their naked hides would not be awaiting them when they got home.

LJ continued to allow his eye to wander about in the church. It caught the stained glass that included an iconography of Jesus. It was through that stained glass that LJ would see a colorful representation of Jesus for the first time. Throughout his life, his mind had been stained and tainted to only see Jesus as a white man like the faces of those he had learned to fear and somewhat worship as what was right within the world. If self-confidence starts within, he needed better representations of people that shared his same melanin. History had a way, specifically in the United States, of whitewashing everything of substance. Leaving the scraps and unapologetic lies to those who've been taught to be submissive and inferior.

Finally sitting down, LJ pulled at the collar of his dress shirt and tugged at his tie. With discomfort on his face and sweat trickling down his spine, he fought the stubborn button, only to feel an aggressive pinch against his skin from the hand of his grandmother. When his eyes caught hers, her wide brown eyes pierced right through his soul. LJ immediately rested his hands in his lap as he dropped his head.

The drummer was setting the tone for the choir. The man sitting on the edge of the pew to LJ's immediate right was stomping his feet. LJ's eyes caught the cloud of floating dust particles as they danced within the streak of light that beamed through the window. The stained glass cast the inside of the church in filtered golden lighting in some areas. It was almost as if it was a halo.

Ever since Bee had told LJ that he needed to be careful and watch his back as Travis and others had it out for them, LJ had been forced to go stay with his grandmother for some of the summer. It was in that church that LJ would spend the bulk of his time. As with any teenager on the verge of the preliminary stages of manhood, church was the last place he wanted to be. LJ had to find some type of solace for his current imprisonment of boredom.

As the riffs from the guitar got stronger, the smile on LJ's grandmother's face spread wider and the claps of her hands grew bigger. She was a beautiful shade of brown. With minimal signs of age on her face, she glowed. Atop her head was her church wig a plum-colored hat.

LJ sighed as his mind continued to wander. What was Bee doing? How was he coping with the potential threat? LJ had sensed a change in Bee the day before he left to stay with his grandmother. Bee's words had become hardened along with his facial expressions. His actions were more aggressive—proactive in nature. He'd begun to smoke more. His ego was beginning to blossom more into the type of nigga no one would want to fuck with—physically. Niggas aren't born, they're developed and conditioned—an idea that would soon be learned and understood. The identification of being a nigga would consume the crab-in-the-barrel mentality that would have a grip on many neighborhoods such as the Low Reign, stagnating growth in the process. LJ sensed the distance that was happening between the two, but a brother he would remain, and he would forever be his brother's keeper.

The preacher was now at the pulpit in the middle of his sermon. He stood before the congregation. Sweat covered his face. He was a rather chunky man with a thick mustache and a processed curl. His wrist was decorated with gold, same as his fingers. He screamed. He yelled. He often sounded like he was hyperventilating, but he seemed to have the spirit in him. People would shout. Some jerking, spinning, leaping into a praise as the Holy Ghost made its rounds.

LJ's eyes were now heavy, and he found it difficult to keep them open. His head fell forward only for him to snap it back abruptly. The preacher had been talking about what it meant to be a man of God. He based his sermon around John 14:6. With a sleepy mind, LJ rationalized that before he could identify and cope with being a man of God, he had to first become a man and for him, that definition was still being shaped.

At the end of service, his grandmother made her rounds, introducing him to everyone she walked past. LJ tended to hear things like: "Is this little LJ? My, has he grown!" "Handsome young man." "Boy, if you don't look like your uncle!" He preferred these statements any day over someone physically pinching his cheek as they used to when he was a chubby kid.

"And LJ, I want to introduce you to—" his grandmother said before he went deaf. LJ stared, not only deaf, but mute. Before him stood the best thing that had happened to him since the service had started. Behind one of the ushers was a girl who stood eye-to-eye with LJ. She was fair skinned with a skinny set of glasses resting on the bridge of her nose. Her cheekbones were defined, and her hair flowed over her shoulders like a falling river. Her body was mature, and she smelled of something sweet, like the inside of his grandmother's kitchen. LJ was smitten.

"LJ don't be rude. Introduce yourself," his grandmother said.

Still at a loss for words as he was lost in the girl's beauty, LJ extended his hand and said something. The girl smiled and met his hand, saying, "Hi. My name is Sandy. Nice to meet you."

Her skin was soft and soon goosebumps had spread all over LJ's body. The usher went on to say that Sandy would be staying with her over the summer as she prepped for her freshman year of college. LJ's grandmother sensed the courtship that rested in his eyes and tugged him along as she said, "Well we'll be seeing y'all. You coming to Wednesday service, Gladys?"

"Of course! Where else would I be? And she's coming too," she said as she covered Sandy's shoulders with her arm.

As they walked out the church LJ whispered to his grandmother, "What time we need to be here by on Wednesday?"

"*We!*" she replied with a twitch of surprise as a chuckle fell from her mouth.

At their vehicle across the street from the church, adjacent to a liquor store, a man with a cleanly shaven face, wearing a white-collared shirt with a red bowtie, approached them. He handed a pamphlet to LJ before his grandmother took it away from him. The man told

LJ that they were God's people and it showed through their passion and spirituality. He told him that they were the lost children of Israel. He called LJ "young brother." He didn't refer to him as 'boy' or 'nigga.' He'd called him his brother. Something in the way it rolled off the man's tongue did more for him in those couple of seconds than sitting in that church had for three hours.

"Don't you pay that nonsense no mind," his grandmother said before tossing the pamphlet in the backseat of the car.

LJ pulled the seatbelt across his chest before asking, "Grandma, why is there always a liquor store by a church? And why are there a row of churches on the same street?"

"You can never have too much of the Lord, LJ. Now hush. No more questions."

As they pulled away, LJ stole another glimpse of the man in the bowtie from the passenger-side mirror. He would eventually pick up the crumpled pamphlet that his grandmother had tossed on the floor in the backseat of her car and read more about what the man had told him.

"You sure you know what you doing?" a boy with dreads in a fade asked Bee. Bee, back resting against a sofa that had been stained over the years, placed his hands behind his head before tilting it up toward the ceiling. He allowed his thoughts to float into the empty space that rested between his ears.

Inside the apartment with only one bedroom, the sounds of a local rap group from Memphis, Eightball and MJG, blasted from the stereo. The residue from the marijuana that had just been rolled atop the black Bible on the coffee table was being wiped into the hands of another young boy who had on a red baseball cap twisted backward.

Even though the sun was blindingly bright outside, the inside of the apartment was darkened by the thick burgundy curtains that covered the front window. The dark cast mirrored the energy in the room as Bee reached for the gun he'd just purchased with the money that Travis had given him at the Southbrook Mall a couple of months ago.

The boy in the red cap asked for the stereo to be turned down as he lifted the remote control, a cloud of smoke rising from his mouth. His arm was inked with images and signs that Bee had often seen on buildings, stop signs and the desks of his classrooms. The lady on the television was talking about a serial killer in Milwaukee known as the Milwaukee Cannibal. The screen became fuzzy with lines and the lady's mouth moved rapidly as the boy in the red cap extended the remote control toward the television. He pressed another button, bringing the television back into focus as two heavyweight boxers danced in the ring. "Mike whooped that boy's ass," he said through a raspy voice.

Bee took pulls from the joint as he focused on his new toy.

"This nigga think he Doughboy or some shit," the dread headed boy said.

Laughter cut through the room.

"Pass that indo," the boy in the red cap demanded. "Your brother was *that* nigga," he continued to Bee. "Mane, he didn't take no shit."

Bee's brother had lost his life in the streets three years prior. He was heavily involved in the game of drugs, with crack being his superior product. Bee didn't talk about his brother much as he only knew one side of him—the caring big brother side who could do no wrong. Bee would only learn about the other side of his brother—that which cost him his life—from the lips of others.

Bee squinted as the curtains were spread wide. The natural light cut across his face, casting the perfect shadow for a portrait, the cut on his face still visible. In the light, one could see more of the tiny apartment: the ceiling fan, with a blown light, hanging from a popcorn ceiling; the makeshift desk underneath the windowsill, housing an assortment of pots with plants sprouting from them; the wicker chair that rested in the corner, not too far from the edge of the desk where the boy in the red hat stretched his wiry legs. In the opposite corner, there was a bookshelf with copies of *Soledad Brother* and *Soul on Ice* facing the front. Pictures of smiling faces covered the walls along with large black iron musical notes. Underneath the pictures sat the television with a VCR on top, and the large stereo and a record player on top of that next to it.

Bee, sitting across from the television, looked on as Mike Tyson and Razor Ruddock continued to exchange blows. He thought about his father. He still hadn't forgiven him for not picking him up on that day when his life had changed. He rationalized that if his father would have been there, he wouldn't have gotten jumped that day. Even when Bee learned why his father hadn't shown up, he still blamed him.

Bee stood and tucked the gun inside his boxers and gym shorts.

"Be careful with that," the boy with the dreads said.

"There is no coming back from this—you know that right?" the boy with the red cap added.

Bee didn't say a word. He just made a face that understood what the implications would be. Bee was high. With his eyes heavy and head cloudy, he dragged his feet to the front door. As he stood in the walkway outside the apartment door, the sun seemed as if it had instantly covered every angle of his body. His shadow was long and lanky against his back legs. He looked over the balcony and glanced at the kids at the playground spinning in circles in the swings. He realized that those days were long gone for him. The innocence of laughter and play no longer resonated with Bee.

Sitting on the steps, Bee rubbed both hands over his head, the tension and anxiety within steadily increasing. Beads of sweat formed on his forehead and the back of his neck. The gun that was tucked inside the waist of his shorts started to feel uncomfortable, but Bee didn't make any adjustments.

He heard the sound of heels clacking against the concrete steps below him. As the sound drew closer,

Bee didn't look up to notice the lady and the girl walking pass him. With his head still hung and his arms resting on his knees, he heard the lady tell the girl, "Don't be looking at no boys." That girl was of no interest to Bee. He continued to sit there lost in his thoughts.

"Yo, you know where that fool be at?" Bee heard through the crack of the front door of the apartment.

Bee nodded.

"Alright—let's ride then, nigga."

Bee exhaled as he clutched the area near his waist before standing. Most of the scarring and bruising on his body was nearly gone. He heard the boy in the red hat greet the woman walking out of the apartment next door with manners he'd never guess would fall from his mouth. He heard the woman ask him about why he no longer attended church. The boy—who had since removed the hat from atop his head—told her he would soon make his way back. They both said their goodbyes. When she was no longer in sight, he asked Bee, "Nigga, you get the bullets?"

Inside the vehicle, more weed was lit and passed around from hand to hand. More bass and treble moved from the speakers. A couple of 'Hey babys' were yelled from the front passenger seat at the girls who piqued their interest. Some, 'What's up niggas' would be heard mutually inside and out.

"You alright back there?"

"I'm good," Bee replied.

The boy with the dreads was driving. His eyes shifted left and right in search of the blue car with the white top and tinted windows.

"You sure this where this nigga hang out at?"

Bee nodded before replying, "Yeah."

"Shit. I can't be out here too much longer. I got to pick my momma up from work," the boy with the dreads said.

The boy in the red hat turned toward the back and stared down Bee. "Where else you think he would be at?"

Bee shrugged his shoulders.

The boy in the red hat rolled his eyes and sighed as he checked his watch. "Fool you best not be late picking up moms. You know how she get to trippin."

As the car turned, Bee stared out at the world. He stared at the passing cars, buildings, and landscape. He felt as if he was in the back of that police car again. Only this time, his father wouldn't be waiting him to take him home. Bee had known the danger that awaited him once he stood from those steps with the gun tucked in his shorts. He knew there wasn't any turning back. Bee could no longer distinguish the voice of his grandfather. He no longer carried around the chess piece that used to be his source of strength. He no longer attended church. No scripture was carried within his heart. His heart was cold and if scriptures did exist, they would currently be on ice.

MEMPHIS CITY BLUES

LJ's legs stretched to the mahogany coffee table as his feet rested across the top, one foot over the other, finding his comfort. As a youth, LJ would often sit in his grandfather's lap when they watched baseball, anything about wildlife and nature, or the Lakers. While in his lap, he would often imitate his grandfather as he, too, used to stretch his legs long and rest his feet on top of the mahogany table, one foot over the other, finding his comfort. Same chair. Same table. Same mannerisms.

LJ prodded his spoon slowly into the bowl which was filled to the rim with a cereal that turned the milk a colorful hue when the cereal turned soggy—just how LJ liked it. He enjoyed the sweet taste of the milk once the cereal was gone.

The bay window in the kitchen welcomed in the morning light, cutting through to the living room, causing a glare against the television screen.

"Grandma!" LJ yelled as drops of milk fell from his mouth. "Ya news bout to come on."

LJ heard the rumble of the kitchen faucet as the water shut off. A neighbor, Mr. Dandridge, would be there soon to look at it. LJ called him his grandmother's boyfriend, which was often met with a rise of his grandmother's cheeks, a blush of her face and a "stop that nonsense" reply.

LJ could hear her slippers shuffling against the tile in the kitchen as she drew near. He caught a whiff of the boldness of the coffee she had brewed. It was strong, no sign of sweetness. LJ made a face, expressing his disdain for her morning pleasure. He'd taken a sip once and it tasted like dirt was being served in a cup. It was almost as bad as the aftertaste of nicotine when he first smoked a cigarette.

She rested one hand against the arm of the couch before slowly taking a seat. She let out a heavy sigh as the steam from her coffee swirled and evaporated against the light. A large family portrait, trimmed with a gold frame, hung above her head.

"What time is your boyfriend coming over?" LJ asked with a smile spread wide across his face.

She turned toward the standing mirror to her right and caught the reflection of herself. She fluffed her hair a little, raised her arm to look at her watch and replied, "LJ, let me alone now. You know that's not my boyfriend." Her cheeks were raised, face hot.

"I shole hope they don't be reporting no more killings this morning." She blew toward the rim of her cup, catching the steam, making it blow every which way—an extension of her breath. "Last night I felt like I was watching an episode of *The Twilight Zone* the way them bodies was popping up on the news."

LJ laughed to match the chuckle of his grandmother.

"Did Puma ever come home last night?"

"No ma'am."

"I got a trick for him tonight. He betta stay where he's at because he not getting in here tonight. He lucky if I keep his clothes in here."

"That's cold, Grandma—that's *cold*."

"That's not cold—*that's* life. If you got a place to rest your head on a Thursday night, you should keep your head on that same pillow on Friday. This ain't no hotel."

The intro for the news came on. The sound and graphic of a steamboat with WMC TV5 Memphis glowed in bright gold. After the voiceover said, "This is action news five," the voice of one of the anchors, a white man, provided an overview of the lead story followed by an attractive black woman anchor giving the remaining details. Another shooting had happened over night, leaving two in critical condition and one dead.

After several "eeem, eeem, eeems" and headshakes from his grandmother, LJ mimicked her with a tease. As a child, he used to do that often to her when she would be on the phone with her "white people's voice" as LJ joked, to her displeasure. As she talked, the telephone cord would stretch far: to the living room, hallway, front door, bathroom... With the phone pressed against her ear and shoulder, she would at times be multitasking, doing other things such as cooking, cleaning, clipping coupons. Often one would hear her say things such as "uh-huh," "no she didn't," "eem, eem, eem" and "bless her heart." Once, LJ had pulled the cord from the phone base and chuckled as his grandmother kept talking into empty air before finally saying 'hello' several times and realizing the line had been cut. That day he caught a whoopin' for interfering in grown folks' business.

After a commercial break, the woman anchor proceeded to discuss the opening of the Civil Rights Museum.

"Finally, something good being reported." She turned toward LJ and for a split second, it was like looking at a younger version of her husband. LJ's broad shoulders, stretched straight, wide, blades defined, just like his grandfather. The way he moved, and his mannerisms reminded her of him. It was a sweet reminder.

"One day before school start back, we are going," she said in LJ's direction.

LJ had the bowl tilted over his mouth, head slightly pulled back, quick thuds coming from his throat. "Going where?" he finally replied.

"To the Civil Rights Museum."

"Aw Grandma... I ain't trying to learn nothing—it's the summer."

"Well, that's probably why you caught up in the mess you in now—because you ain't trying to *learn* nothing."

LJ shook his head.

"I don't know what's wrong with you young folk. It's like the city been cursed ever since Dr. King was assassinated."

"Times different now, Grandma."

"Ain't nothing new under the sun, except a new level of stupidity." She shook her head and continued, "Then again, I guess you don't know what you don't know."

LJ's grandmother had a blank gaze about her face. "Do you know that the reason Dr. King came down here was to help your grandfather?"

"What you mean?"

She went on to tell LJ that as a former sanitation worker, his grandfather, who was forty-three at the time, had to endure such injustices as being paid less than two-dollars an hour, not getting paid for overtime, no uniforms and not being able to take showers, which were luxuries his white counterparts had.

"What do you mean no showers?" LJ asked, eyes wide, gaze focused.

"Back then, as sanitation workers, they sometimes had to work in crazy conditions that often left a smell I can still remember to this day. The white folk was able to clean themselves up before coming home, but black folks had to go as is."

LJ shook his head in disgust.

"I woulda—"

"You wouldna' did nothing but what your grandfather did. He was so young and had life all in his eyes, but I seen it taking something away from him that I didn't know how to fix. You see, I was still young myself with the children at home. I used to hate the sight of that orange truck."

"What happened then?"

"Ol' Henry Loeb, who was the mayor back then, was making it hard with his deep cowlicks ridin' to the back of his ol' cone head and annoying voice. Sound like he was holding his nose up like a pig's snout. He was just stubborn as he wanted to be. Him and Frank Holloman."

She went on to tell LJ about the death of Echol Cole and Robert Walker being crushed in the garbage compactor which led to the strike. She told him what part his family played during that time period. His mother being part of SCLC during her brief stint in college. His father being part of an activist group called The Invaders. LJ's shoulders straightened and his eyes bucked when he learned how much of an activist his father was.

"My dad did all that?" LJ asked, eyes wide.

She stood. "There's a lot about your dad that you don't know."

"Why nobody ever told me?"

"I don't know, LJ. He got his reasons, I guess. Maybe he doesn't want you to think of the world as it was, but as it could be. Those were painful times, maybe he don't like to think about it."

LJ's back rested against the soft cushion of the recliner chair. He pushed his feet against the edge of the table as he slowly rocked, allowing his mind to drift and think about the man he called 'Dad.' There was another layer that he'd never known, a layer that LJ wanted to explore more, to learn who he was before he was his dad.

"What time is *Ms. Sandy* picking you up?" she asked, breaking the silence, stretching her vowels and dancing her eyes.

"Around eleven," LJ replied with a jolt of interest.

"Uhm, hmm. I *see* the way you look at her," she continued to tease.

"Aw, Grandma. It's not like that. Besides, she about to go to college and I already got a girlfriend."

"*And* I see the way she looks at you too!"

LJ sat in silence and folded his arms across his chest. His feet were now planted firmly against the carpeted floor. When he was younger, he would often think about the day when his feet would no longer dangle into empty space as he sat in the recliner, back against the cushion, rocking away, force created by his arms and back.

After a couple of seconds with his thoughts, LJ yelled out, "*How* does she look at me?

All he heard was the sound of her slippers shuffling against the tile in the kitchen, the clink of her cup being placed in the sink, and the flick of the hallway light. It was time for her to get dressed for the faucet to be fixed.

LJ lay across the bed, hand over his stomach, taste buds still tingling from the hot wings he'd just eaten. He listened as Sandy's feet pounded against the floor, hands clapping, fingers snapping. She was listening to Bell Biv Devoe's latest song called "Poison."

As LJ continued to lay across the colorful floral comforter, he caught a whiff of the sweet scent that Sandy carried with her. The scent was fruity, as if she would taste like candy if he could get a bite. He turned his head to steal a glimpse of her dancing. She was wearing some black biking shorts with a pink streak in the middle. Her t-shirt, which had a celebrity's face on the front, was tied in a knot, making it easier for LJ to see the roundness and curves of her fully developed body at the top and bottom. He continued to stare. He saw the sweat rolling down the back of her neck, her hair sticking to her neck in certain places. She would flick out her tongue during certain moves when she would poke her backside out and her breast would jiggle inside her shirt. LJ felt his pants tighten.

Sandy reached for her glass of water that was sitting atop her nightstand. A stack of envelops from different schools rested next to the glass, some open, some not. The flowers she had received for graduation or prom had withered inside the glass vase next to her lamp which had no shade attached to it. A poster of MC Hammer was thumbtacked to the wall that was scarred with crayon, pencil and ink pen marks.

"So, you just gonna lay there and not dance with me?" she asked LJ with her lips wet. She pulled her hair back, forming a ponytail.

"I told you I couldn't dance."

She blew air from her mouth, still trying to catch her breath. She sat next to LJ, her buttocks a couple of inches from his head. "Have you talked to Keisha lately?" she asked him. LJ's brows danced in bewilderment.

"Who is Keisha?" LJ replied.

She raised one of her legs to pull off the thick colorful socks she had been wearing, exposing her bare feet. LJ caught the sour smell, but it wasn't the type that would make you cover your nose. The smell was still sweet in a way, at least to LJ it was.

"Are you talkin' bout my girlfriend Krystal?" LJ asked, brows knitted together.

"Oh, *that's* her name. I'll try to remember next time," she replied, words dripping with sarcasm.

LJ hadn't developed enough to understand what she was really asking. He still hadn't grasped the game of courtship. The truth was, ever since LJ had begun to interact with Sandy, he'd been thinking less and less about Krystal. The two weeks he's been at his grandmother's house has been sort of a detox for LJ. Not only had he been able to rid some of the inner toxins, he'd also lost some of the luster for the good things in his life that were happening as well. It was like he was living a double life.

"Are you excited about college?" LJ asked.

Sandy maneuvered her body to lay next to LJ. They both stared at the ceiling. Sandy's shirt had come untied and was raised just shy of her breast, stomach exposed, flat with a tenderness to it. "In a way, but I'm going to miss my friends."

"I can't wait to leave high school and be on my own," LJ said.

"Are you really going back home this evening?" Sandy asked. Her voice was low, almost as if she were disappointed at the thought. The words cut through LJ as well. He felt an emptiness inside. He didn't respond.

"You know we probably won't ever see each other again," she continued.

They both turned toward one another, catching eyes. The smell of her breath, the glare of her eyes, the thickness of her lips…it made LJ hot all over his body. LJ lay stiff like a stone. A smile formed on Sandy's face. It was slow and seductive. She allowed her hand to smooth over his face to his kinky hair, toying within the coils. One of her fingers grazed over his lips, pulling open his bottom lip somewhat. She continued to stare down the boy who was two years her junior, yet he had something about him that she wanted to take while she had the opportunity. He was still sweet and honest in his way. The boy hadn't been hardened yet by society's expectations about manhood. He'd yet to develop that aggressive and disrespectful boldness the boys she'd been used to dealing with had grown into. LJ had a tenderness about his eyes. He often chose his words carefully. They were soft and had an innocent truthfulness about them—maybe due to being inexperienced. He'd opened doors for her, offered to pay for lunch, put gas in the car and watched her dance without trying to grab her ass or make juvenile references about her anatomy.

Sandy was now close enough to steal a kiss from LJ. His mouth welcomed hers. She climbed on top of him, pulled her shirt from over her head, unhooked her bra and allowed her breasts to be in his view. She pulled his hands toward them and showed him how to cup them. LJ would go on to lose his virginity that afternoon to the girl he would never see again. He believed he'd reached a new level of manhood.

No tears trailed from Bee's eyes to his pillow. He was void of emotion. The dark blue bath towel draped over his curtain, blocking the unwanted light, except for around the edges where the stubborn sun outlined his window. With his hands tucked behind the untidy coils of his hair, fingers interlocked, he continued to have flashbacks of the night before. His clothing was still soiled and reeked of marijuana, while the smell of alcohol fumed from his mouth. The calmness within each breath that he took was too cool, too natural, too normalized. He had become hardened in his own way overnight. The streets whispered into the pull of his ear an alternate version of manhood—a version that left two young men in critical condition and one dead.

The night had started off as any other summer night for Bee and some of his new friends. The sound of insects chirping and buzzing against the thick humidity in the air. The smell of charcoal flowing from various backyards. Kids laughed in the streets as they gasped for air from their latest game.

Bee stood, back resting against the light pole, the glow casting against his dark skin, highlighting the hair that had formed under his chin. His hair was no longer curly to perfection, he'd since favored an unkempt look, so no comb touched his hair. His features were harder, rougher about the face. He took another pull from the cigarette before reaching into his shorts to pull out his new beeper. A young man with a circular face and soft eyes pulled out a plastic bag that had what looked like tiny yellowish stones in the corner of it. He handed it to Bee. Cars would drive by every so often with bass rattling trunks. Some stopped, others went by and in others, necks would stretch out and yell 'what up' or 'get buck,' buck being stretched to "buuuck."

Bee stared into the night, reading faces, remembering movements on the corner. Paranoia caused his eyes to dance. He was more cautious with his words. He was learning a new level of codes and respect within the streets. The same streets that nurtured his brother and led his father into prison. It was the same streets where he took a beating, played as a kid, learned to fight and dreamed.

A white car with gold trimming and rims to match pulled up slowly at the corner. Bee's friend with the red baseball cap was in the passenger seat. He extended his hand toward Bee and they completed a handshake reserved only for those who had the privilege of it.

"What's up, nigga? You trying to ride out?"

Bee looked toward the boy with the circular face. The boy sucked his teeth and said, "That's your money you'll be losing."

Bee pulled out the stash that was tucked within his shorts and allowed his fingers to flick through the money he'd earned for the day. He told his friends he'd be back before the night was over.

After passing around multiple marijuana joints, taking swigs of St. Ides and allowing crude jokes and catcalls to spill from their mouths, the boys pulled into a fast-food burger restaurant, seeking to fulfill their appetite. They all lingered in the car, slurring their words, but then they finally exited. A cloud of smoke rose from their doors like steam coming from an enclosed shower. They laughed and joked their way to the front door in between head turns toward the women exiting the restaurant. More whistles and demeaning words spilled from their mouths. The rowdy and confident group of boys who were at the peak of their high and testosterone stood in line, still laughing and joking, waiting to order their food. Another group of young men walked in, mirroring their energy. They were riding their own level of highness and testosterone.

The boy in the backward red hat stared down the group of boys. He rolled his eyes and whispered to Bee that he didn't like the way one of them looked at him. The other group of boys began their own whispering. A stare down ensued until someone blurted out, "What the fuck you looking at?" Chaos followed.

It took fifteen minutes before all parties involved were asked to leave the property. No cops were called. It was a typical occurrence. More testosterone had been built up within Bee and his friends. More marijuana was lit up. More aggressive music massaged their emotions. Night kept falling.

As they turned the corner heading back to drop Bee off again, the driver of the car screamed, "There them niggas go right there!" The boy in the red cap threw his hat to the floor, exposing a low-cut fade. His eyes were dark. Profanity rolled from his tongue in Bee's direction. Everything was happening in what seemed like warp speed. Bee only heard the words "You ready nigga?" come to his ear. The car sped up; windows rolled down. Bee, riding the wave of his ego, thought about the night he got jumped. Adrenaline. The day his grandfather died. Sadness. The morning his dad didn't show to pick him up. Anger. His mother. Abandonment. LJ. Envy. Being rejected by girls. Self-hatred. The world that once lived within his mind was no more. There was no elusive place for him to simply be Bee. There would be no chess tournaments with him the victor. There would be no smiles spreading across his parents' faces from something he did. Nobody really cared. The world didn't care. People didn't care. God didn't care. Bee didn't like the reflection of the face in the mirror, so he couldn't care less about the black bodies outside that window.

Bee closed his eyes and squeezed. Upon opening them, Bee saw a blinding glare like fire followed by the same deafening sound he'd heard several times before. The only difference was that it was now coming from his hand, which was warm. The aftermath: two boys in critical condition and one dead. He, too, had reached a new level of manhood.

THE RISING SON

The smell of fresh cut grass and gasoline wafted from across the iron fence. A man pushing a lawn mower waved as he maneuvered in the opposite direction. The overbite of the sun stretched wide and sunk its teeth into those who were brave enough to be in the elements. The man continued to push, feet trudging through the thickness of the lawn, shoes caked with stains, mud and grass. A soiled white towel draped from just above his eyes and down the back of his neck, tucked underneath the baseball cap that fit snug on his head. His stomach, the result of daily canned beer and a steady diet of processed foods, overlapped the elastic of his pants. The man stopped, lifted the towel and wiped his forehead, mower still roaring. He fished for air. With a dry swallow, he proceeded to push. Stubborn weeds still lined the edges of the fence that separated his yard from the Johnsons'. Lorenzo had pleaded with the man the week before to do something about his lawn as it was becoming an eyesore. He'd threatened to call the city about the public nuisance. Not to mention the potential for bugs or snakes to lurk inside the small forest of overgrown weeds. Lorenzo also asked him to do something about the large tree branch that was beginning to lean over the fence, which could snap any day and damage the already flimsy fence. The man, now standing on his back porch, tilted his head back as the cool from the canned beer quenched his thirst.

Lorenzo told LJ to turn his body and pivot his feet as sweat fell from his brows. LJ's feet pressed firmly against the manicured lawn, still wet from the watering. Each time LJ threw a punch into the hands of Lorenzo, his body would tighten, more than it used to. The sound of an *umph* would slip from Lorenzo's mouth. LJ was gaining strength. "Maintain your stance and balance," he went on to say. LJ shifted his weight into his right leg. Lorenzo pushed LJ and told him to keep his elbows down and hands up. Lorenzo's body glistened against the sun, exposing some areas of softness as his body moved, his fat free to jiggle with no restrictions. His body was no longer the cut of his younger years, but he was still in good physical shape. "Relax and breathe," he gasped to LJ, wiping the sweat from his eyes with his forearms.

LJ stood firm, elbows down, hands up and chin

tucked just like his dad had told him. Heat against his back, his feet began to shuffle quickly, causing some areas of the grass to bend and fall, creating deep tracks as he yelled out that he was the greatest.

It had been some years since Lorenzo and LJ had boxed in the backyard. When LJ was younger, he'd sit in the living room with his gloves on, watching the clock, looking out the blinds, anticipating his dad returning from his warehouse job. LJ would spend his time watching Rocky movies, fighting the air, wet tissue in his mouth acting as a mouthpiece. Lorenzo would walk in, thank God for allowing him to make it home and for keeping his family safe and sound. He would take one of his large hands and massage LJ's head before walking over to Betty, who would usually be in the kitchen around that time, prepping dinner, talking on the phone, watering her plants or tending to the needs of baby Robbie, and he would playfully smack her across her backside. A kiss would bless her cheek then lips. Lorenzo would pull out a chair from the table with fatigue on his face. He would ask Betty how her day was and if there was anything, he could do to assist with what she had going on. She would say no, and he would then drag his feet toward the door, body aching, mentally drained and tell his son to come outside to box, because he knew that it was the highlight of his son's day. It was during these sessions that they would bond and discuss things that were usually shied away from at the dinner table. Manly things.

"Don't forget to exhale when you punch," he told LJ. After LJ leaned into his power for a jab, he dropped his hands. Sweat covered his face. He fought to catch his breath, trying hard to breathe through his nose like his dad had taught him. Lorenzo dropped his hands encased in black boxing mitts and told LJ that it was enough for now. With his shoulders slumped and his back hunched over, Lorenzo walked to the wrought iron table to grab some bottles of water. He placed his hand over his eyes to shade the brightness of the sun, looking in the direction of the yard behind his house. Lorenzo shook his head, irritated at the way the man was cutting the grass. "Well at least he's cutting it," he whispered to himself, one brow raised.

LJ stood next to Lorenzo, still inches shorter, but the deficit was shrinking as the days and months passed. Lorenzo's shoulders were now square, straight as the perfect jab. LJ squared himself up, squeezing his core, shoulders straight, like his dad.

"I can't believe I'm this tired," LJ said as he squirted some fluid into his mouth.

"It's all about your conditioning. *You* eating a whole package of cookies is not doing you any favors neither," Lorenzo said as he nudged his son in the belly.

"I'm not the one getting rolls," LJ replied, returning the nudge to Lorenzo's belly.

They laughed.

LJ stretched his long and lean frame as Lorenzo skipped and jumped to an imaginary rope, his shadow stretched over the yard. He asked LJ if he was excited about his first year of high school. LJ nodded and proceeded to tell him that he didn't expect much to change. Lorenzo told LJ that times changed everything, including people. Lorenzo asked him about girls, and if he had thoughts about sex. LJ smiled with his lips closed, his secret making his face blush—sweet memories, pleasant reminder.

The sun seemed to beam brighter, harder and more direct. Memphis heat was a different kind of heat. The only comparison was the heat of the delta. LJ sat atop the table, removed his shirt and placed it over his head, but there was no escaping the heat that was chasing them. The rays from the sun sank more into their skin, leaving its mark, a darker shade of their natural hue.

Lorenzo, still moving his body, trying to stay lose to keep his back from stiffening, shadowboxed against the wind. "How are things with you and Bee?" he asked through breaks of breath. "I haven't seen him around lately."

LJ, still trying to fight the heat, repositioned his body, attempting to catch some shade from their next-door neighbor's tree, but the branches didn't extend long enough, partly due to Lorenzo's desire to trim the edges to prevent it from overlapping his yard. "We cool. I guess he just been busy that's all." His smile was now gone. It was replaced by the stillness of his face, straight line of his lips and emptiness about his eyes—the hardened teenager.

Lorenzo pulled up a chair and sat. The chair was hot, and it stung his inner legs. "I seen him not too long ago. He was walking up toward the corner. I don't think he seen me, but something didn't look right."

Lorenzo studied LJ's face. It was a tactic Officer Johnson used during interrogations.

Silence fell between them. LJ sighed as he squinted. The man that was mowing his lawn was now raking the grass into piles to be placed in large garbage bags and hauled off to the curb. LJ looked on. His brows now pinched tight together, the bridge of his nose slightly raised. He expected a lecture to follow about his poor choices in friends and how it would one day catch up to him. He wished they were still boxing so that he could slip a punch to Officer Johnson's chin, like he did when he was younger, but this time it wouldn't be an accident and there would be power behind it.

Lorenzo stood and placed a hand on his son's shoulder and said, "I was wrong to say that. Bee is a good kid and a good friend, but I'm just saying he didn't look himself. Just keep an eye out for him and be careful… That's all I'm saying." Lorenzo dropped his head, searching for more words that would rekindle their bonding moment.

LJ beat him to the punch. "Why you never told me you fought with Dr. King and went to jail?"

Lorenzo's eyes widened. "Where did you hear that from? Your *mom*?"

LJ shook his head. "No. Grandma Anna."

A snicker followed by a sigh fell from Lorenzo's mouth as he replied, "Shoulda known that. What all did she tell you?"

"Enough," LJ replied, eyes still squinted straight ahead, the risen sun illuminating his melanin. The man who was mowing his lawn was no longer in sight. The weeds still lined the fence. "She told me that you got caught busting a window, fighting with a cop. Went to jail."

Lorenzo's face was tight. He wasn't fearful of being viewed as a hypocrite in terms of his actions at that age. His fight was a plausible one. You couldn't compare the two situations. But he was wise enough to understand to choose and pick certain battles, so he deferred.

"Well, I wouldn't necessarily call it fighting *with* him. *For* him? Yes. But not with him. I never met him. I had some peers who did, but *me*…I never actually met the man." Staring at the weeds opposite his fence, face still tight, he continued, "My peers—sorry—my *friends* at that time were what one would call revolutionary. I chose them and would have walked through fire for them."

LJ listened.

"I don't know why I don't speak on it much. I guess I just assumed accountability and responsibility for my actions and moved on from it. I was angry, rebellious and immature in some ways. I *hated* the police. Hated is probably not a strong enough word for my feelings at the time. To be honest with you, that's the reason why I decided to be a cop. We needed more of our faces to balance the scale. I didn't want the next generation coming up to have that same fear and anger toward the police. But I guess my plan didn't work out too well…huh?"

LJ didn't respond; he just continued to look straight ahead. He wasn't judging his father. He just wanted to know more about the younger version of the man that stood beside him. He wanted to know more about the decisions he'd made and why he made them. He wanted to know more about the circle of friends that he had run with. He wanted to know how they ended up. He wanted to know if the mistakes his dad had made as a youth had shaped him to be the man that he was today, why couldn't he allow LJ to do the same? No more words escaped their lips because Lorenzo received a page that seemed to be urgent based on his facial expression. Officer Johnson was back on duty. LJ sat, still beaming like the sun hanging against the ocean blue sky with waves of thick white clouds riding the currents of the wind.

Krystal, legs dangling below the back of LJ's mother's car, bit into her candy apple, her hands sticky from the drippings of its sweetness. She no longer wore braces and she enjoyed the newfound freedom of being able to enjoy every taste that piqued her interest. Her hair was no longer braided together. She now wore it in a long ponytail that draped over her shoulder. She extended the candy apple to LJ, offering him another chance to taste its bliss. LJ shook his head in silence.

"Why did you stop calling me?" she asked, legs still swinging freely.

LJ sat next to her. His legs hung down, no movement, straight, firm, almost as if his feet were planted against the ground. He wanted her to recognize that he was a man now. He would be sixteen in a week's time, but he'd grown so much in the three weeks since they'd last seen each other. He wanted her to recognize the extra hairs that sprouted over his lip. Didn't she notice the deepness of his voice? The square of his shoulders? The swing of his walk? The halo of cool that floated above his head? Did she notice that he was no longer a virgin? Could she smell the masculinity of his cologne, the whiff of childhood innocence no longer existing? Did she notice?

LJ hunched his shoulders as he stared out into the street. His neighbors were planting flowers, Mrs. King and her son Mario, his hands that would be developed for writing digging deep into the flesh of the earth, soil under his nails. A couple houses down, Toya, LJ's younger brother's crush, was hauling a small bag of dirt from one area to the next. Yard work on a Saturday was like water to the body for Memphians. It was a necessity for life.

Krystal stared straight ahead as well. She wanted LJ to notice how she, too, had changed. Didn't he notice the extra pop of her lip gloss? The maturity of her hair? Boldness of her tongue? Glare in her eyes? She, too, had occupied her time with someone. The cute boy that lived next door to her grandmother. He was a year younger, but he was "mature" for his age. She'd bragged to her friends about how his eyes made her want to melt into his arms. How the curl of his hair was the perfect complement to his smooth skin which was shades lighter than LJ's. How they'd kissed repeatedly on the wooden swing by the park. They would touch parts of each other's body, exploring the curiosity of their pleasures. However, they would stop at that. Neither were bold enough to go beyond.

Another bite, the sound of the crunch and mush of the apple breaking the awkward silence. She leaped from the trunk of the car, flip flops slapping against the concrete. With the stick from the candy apple wedged in between her teeth, she picked up her bike, waved her hand at LJ and rode into the rays of the sun. LJ stared until she was no longer in view, regret on his face and words he should have said forming on his tongue. His body wanted to leap from the hood of the car and go after her, but something inside him wouldn't allow him to. He would learn that the feeling was his male ego and it would cause him more harm than good. They would soon break up and get back together—the typical teen-aged love affair.

Still staring out into the street, LJ saw his father coming up the street, but the car stopped. LJ's eyes widened. He leaned over, stretched his neck, before leaping off the hood of the car. Officer Johnson stepped out of his vehicle and walked up the driveway to Bee's house. He was knocking at the door.

Bee struggled to push his body from the ground, arms wobbly, muscles fatigued, as tears fell from his eyes. He'd spent the last twenty minutes doing push-ups and sit-ups, gathering his strength from the inner hurt and pain that had been masked by anger. It was an anger that darkened his heart. It was an anger that made him feel more alive with the rising of the moon and falling of the sun. His days were the night and his nights were the day. Darkness allowed him to be void of his emotions. Somehow his problems could easily be tucked away underneath the comfort of the blanket of the night, when others were sleeping. Their eyes couldn't see his pain. He could easily shy away from the caring and curious eyes of those who wanted to question his whereabouts, like his mother. He could easily slip past friends who'd left him messages on the answering machine that said, "Yo, Bee, I'll be back home today, and I got something crazy to tell you," like his friend LJ. The formalities of happiness were no longer of interest to him, because he knew the truth and fate that awaited him. There was no escape. Bee was depressed.

Earlier that morning, before the sun had risen and when the wind still had a coolness to it, Bee and his mother Tammy had driven to visit Charles in prison. Tammy had been asking Charles to allow Bee to come on the next visit as she was concerned. Charles had rejected her, saying that he didn't want his son to see him that way. Not any longer. Charles was battling his own depression—a depression of regret. He regretted not being the father that Bee needed and wanted. He regretted being another link in the chain of the prison pipeline, instead of breaking it. He regretted being the man that he was but was optimistic about the man he was becoming. He'd spent nights on his cot, eyes closed, thinking about his son's eyes. He'd remembered the innocence in them. It was the same innocence that he once knew, until he was hardened by the fallacies of manhood.

With conviction in her voice, choking on her words, Tammy had pleaded with Charles. She had told him about the shoebox that was full of cash underneath his bed. She knew that it didn't come from cutting yards. She no longer found soiled and stained clothing in the hamper from that line of work. Bee's clothes now carried a musty smell or of smoke, like most of the corner boys she'd known over the years. She told him how he would often come home drunk or high off god-knows-what. She knew Bee's eyes and the eyes she'd been witnessing as of late wore a look that was all too familiar to her. She too recognized the error of her ways. Bee was becoming the product of his environment. They cheated him into manhood before he was ready and fully developed. They denied him his chance at growing and becoming the peace within the continuous storm. Charles agreed.

Bee sat across the table, head down, eyes at his feet. Charles sat in his chair, jumpsuit matching the others. Bee heard Charles mutter something, but he couldn't make it out clearly. The room carried a heavy echo. Inmates were making the most of their time, saying their last words before goodbyes. All those voices floated into Bee's focus. Bee finally made out the words Charles had been saying and lifted his head. When their eyes caught, the sting in the back of Bee's throat made it hard for him to speak. He had become too manly to allow his words to choke.

"I was wrong." The words became clearer. "I was wrong, son."

Sometimes it's hard to change before the eyes who once knew who you were. Eyes that were able to judge you by what they've seen. Charles understood that. He knew how his words could very easily fall on deaf ears. His track record spoke for itself, but he had always been a man of conviction, whether right or wrong. If he could stand still and firm within his wrongs, he should be strong enough to carry that same weight for something that was right. He knew his son didn't belong in the world that he'd found himself in. He knew underneath that hardened exterior, there was a child that was still soft. It was the type of softness that he regretted once calling weak. It was a softness that could potentially save his life.

"I heard about your friend—what was his name?"

"He wasn't my friend," Bee replied, straight-faced and slouched in his chair.

"What was his name though?" Charles asked, curiosity about his eyes.

"Freddie."

"That's right—Freddie! The fat kid, right?"

Bee nodded.

"How's the other two kids—Travis and Ant?"

Bee hunched his shoulder. He shielded his eyes from Charles.

"You wouldn't happen to know anything about that—right?" Charles asked, staring straight through his son, searching for the answers that the streets had been gossiping.

Bee shook his head. He stood and stared down at the man who'd caused some of the pain that he'd been feeling. He stared at the jumpsuit that matched the other men who were paying for the choices they'd made, trying to make amends for it. He realized that they all were chess pieces on a board. Bee just didn't know the type of piece he was. The anger that was still in him spilled out into his words as he told Charles that he couldn't tell him shit. He'd told him that it was too late. He didn't allow a tear to fall from his eye. He walked into the direction of the door and didn't turn around to see his father weeping into his hands.

Bee's body flopped unto the floor, no strength in his arms to do another push-up. The sound of the doorbell followed by a couple of knocks startled him. He hadn't been expecting anyone. His paranoia had grown following that night when his hand was warm from the gun. He struggled to his feet and slowly walked near the door, only to stop. He crouched down and leaned close to the window that provided a full view of the street and driveway. His heart accelerated at the sight of the police car. No sirens. No flashing lights. He closed his eyes and let out a sigh, flashes of that night in his vision. His grandfather had once told him that the sun and moon were the eyes of God. Always watching. All-seeing. He'd told him that there was no escape as whatever is done in the dark will always come to the light. Bee had asked him once, "What about what happens in the light? Will the dark find it?" His grandfather had replied, "The light shines in the darkness and Jesus is that light. If you follow him, then darkness will not find you. Just keep rising, son."

ENTRAPMENT

Outside, the breath of summer's wrath was suffocating the locals, trapping them under the wave of her heat. Kids with different textured coils atop their heads searched for relief in the flow of lukewarm water from garden hoses. Others chased down their friends with the hoses as they pressed their thumbs against the male end of it, causing a forceful gush of water to shower their prey. Aspiring rappers drove around the city with their windows down, hoping to catch a breeze, in pursuit of selling their latest tape out of the trunk of their cars. Boys whose faces where ashy from the sweat that had dried sat under the shade of trees and yelled out "That's my car" toward the vehicles that caught their eyes. Young girls sat under carports, trading candies and talking about the latest boy groups on the covers of magazines, fanning their faces as their hair stuck to their necks, pulling out the extended posters to post on their walls. Mothers could be heard screaming things like, "You come in here again—you are staying in," "Close that door," or "You smell like outside."

This was a typical summer in the Low Reign.

Inside, LJ was sitting at the dinner table with his family. He sat, long in the face, dancing his fork around the vegetables on his plate, face cuffed into the palm of his hand. Across from LJ sat Robbie, feet sturdy on the ground due to his growth spurt during the summer. He lightly pounded his fist against the dinner table as he mouthed rhyming words and sentences in rhythm with his beat. A group of entangled rubber bands hung from his neck, imitating a gold rope, and a four-finger ring made of paper wrapped his hand. Betty, back straight against her chair, chewed slowly, eyes closed, cherishing each bite. Lorenzo hunched over his plate, like a dog protecting his bowl of food, working his jaws, he, too, enjoying the flavor of every bite.

Eating dinner together at the table as a family was something that Lorenzo and Betty had set as a non-negotiable. After Betty yelled, "Time to eat," LJ and Robbie would often drag their feet to the table with pinched eyebrows, lips poked out with inflated jaws, especially if they were presented with meals that consisted of vegetables or the worst meat known to mankind—liver. The bland and bitter taste of it would make their stomachs churn of regret. Lorenzo's and Betty's eyes would often roam across and around the table, feeling a sense of thankfulness and appreciation. LJ and Robbie's eyes would be cast downward, feeling trapped, as if they were missing something vital that was happening outside their four walls with their friends. But in due time, sitting at that dinner table would shape the memories of their childhood in priceless ways.

"So LJ, what do you think about the Penny Hardaway kid playing for the Tigers this season? Is he as good as everyone is saying?" Lorenzo asked, fork in hand and jaws still working.

LJ, still dancing his fork around his vegetables while resting his face against his fist, mouthed a low and unenthused, "Best in the city."

Lorenzo wiped his mouth with a paper towel, chewing the last remains of the food. He swallowed before replying, "Best in the city, huh?"

"I'm excited about the Pyramid they're building. I can't wait until it opens in the fall," Betty interrupted. She'd returned from her weekly visit to the beauty shop and her hair was a set of bouncing curls. A paper towel, smeared with the lipstick that was once on her lips, rested in her lap. Her eyes cut toward Robbie and she continued, "Enough beating already. Who do you think you are? LL Fool J?" Smiles and chuckles rounded the table. Even LJ had to break his hard exterior for a second. LJ and Robbie were always amused when either one of their parents would reference anyone in their genre of music.

"Is *somebody* ready for their big day tomorrow?" Betty asked in LJ's direction. A wide smile stretched across her face.

"I guess so," LJ replied.

"You *guess* so!" Lorenzo repeated as he leaned back into his chair. His undershirt was snug on his body. The smell of the street still fresh on his skin. "You mean to tell me after all this hoopla you been raising since you were thirteen about how you couldn't wait until you turned sixteen and now that you're a day away—all you got to say is 'I *guess* so?'" Lorenzo chuckled and continued, "Teens—*boy,* I tell ya."

"Let him be, Lorenzo. He's just acting his age. We *all* were crazy around this time in our lives," Betty said as she stood to place her and Lorenzo's plates in the sink.

"Baby, I'll wash 'em," Lorenzo said.

"That's okay. I got it—dessert?"

Lorenzo patted his hand atop his protruding belly and replied, "Well of course." He then pulled a small box wrapped in red gift paper out of his pocket and placed it in front of LJ. LJ's hand reached for it before Lorenzo pulled it back. "Not until tomorrow—promise?" he said with a raised brow.

LJ nodded. "Yeah. Promise."

Betty placed a bowl of Jell-O on the table. An assortment of fruit lined the edges. The gelatin delight wiggled and danced, multiple spoons extending from the bowl.

She exhaled as she sat. "*So*—everybody got their question ready?"

In the Johnson household, everyone had to come to the table with at least one open-ended question toward the end of dinner. It was a tradition that Lorenzo carried over from his childhood. It forced communication. Even during times when communicating was the last thing one may have wanted to do, you had to participate. This was another one of Lorenzo and Betty's nonnegotiables. When LJ or Robbie's friends would stay over for dinner, they would often sit at the table wide-eyed, smiles spread across their faces, engaging in ways that LJ and Robbie would often be embarrassed about. They would tell LJ and Robbie that they wished they did that at home with their family. LJ would get tired of hearing how lucky he was, or that he had fun parents. LJ didn't feel so lucky and there was nothing fun about being forced to eat vegetables or talk.

"Who first?" Betty asked.

Robbie led the way by firing off his question, "How come Jesus can't be black?" He leaned back, waiting for his answer. His arms tucked and crossed over his chest. Robbie didn't share his father's Egyptian eyes like LJ. His were more round around the edges like his mother.

"Who said he's not?" Betty asked as she studied the faces at the table.

"Well, he looks white to me," Robbie added.

"Nobody knows for sure what his color is Robbie." Lorenzo said. "I guess it would be kinda cool if he was black though," he continued as a smile cut his face. "Imagine the faces of some of those racist white folks, when *if* they get to heaven and they see a black man sitting at the throne."

"It would be comedy at its best," Betty added as she chuckled into her hand.

"What you think LJ?" Lorenzo asked.

LJ thought about the pamphlet that he'd retrieved from the back of his grandmother's car after church that Sunday when he'd first met Sandy. He'd been reading more about why and how Christianity wasn't the true religion for black folk.

"I don't know what I think," LJ said straight-faced. "I guess it would be kinda cool if he was. I mean, he would be more relatable."

"Imagine Jesus sitting on the throne with a curl or fade on his head—because you know Jesus *gotta* be keeping up with the times if he's black ya see," Lorenzo said as he leaned over his bowl of Jell-O. His head worked the table as he continued, "His black skin radiant and shining like gold, his clothes *clean* as a whistle. He's slumped down in the throne, cool as the other side of the pillow—and he slaps you five as you make it to heaven—and the first thing he says to you as you make it to the big party in the sky called heaven is, 'Did you bring some potato salad, because white folk shole don't know how to make it. No season or flavor at all. And let's not talk about the macaroni.'"

Everyone at the table fell into a deep laugh. Betty reached over and slapped Lorenzo's arm and said,

"You're too silly. That *would* be a sight to see though."

As the laugher slowed down, Betty said, "I got one." She leaned into the table. "Where do you see yourselves in five years?"

Everyone studied each other's face at the table. Silence fell upon them as they allowed their thoughts to roam.

"I'll start this one," Lorenzo said, breaking the silence. "In *five* years—*damn* that would make me a young fifty-two years old." Lorenzo scratched his chin which was sprinkled with shades of gray hair, still deep in thought. "You know what, I could see these black hands wrapped around the steering wheel of a Lamborghini."

"As long as I'm on the passenger side, that's fine with me," Betty added.

"I'll be old enough to drive by then," Robbie said. "Besides, you'll probably be too old and wrinkled to drive a car that fast."

Lorenzo turned toward LJ. He stared at the face that mirrored his own. There was so much promise and curiosity about the world in his son's eyes. The rebellion and disdain of his actions was nothing more than his manhood trying to swallow his boyhood whole, digesting any remains of an imaginative freedom that existed within his mind. It was a feeling that Lorenzo understood all too well. His manhood was shaped by the society of his times. He witnessed men walk the streets with signs hanging from their necks with words that said, 'I am a man,' as if their manhood didn't exist to the world. It was a world that once said that the manhood that resided underneath black skin was only worth three-fifths. It was a world that rushed young black boys to stretch out of their skin into the cloth of manhood before they were ready. It was a world that reminded them that they weren't men at all, stunting their growth in life to make them boys for the rest of their lives. Lorenzo often wondered what type of world his sons would face as men. How would his sons' manhood be defined?

LJ sat back against his chair, shoulders squared, chest out. He realized in five years he would be twenty-one. As he stared out into the eyes at the dinner table awaiting his answer, a sudden sadness cast over him. As he concentrated on an answer that was manhood-worthy, he realized he didn't have one. All this time he'd been thinking about escaping the four walls of his parents' home, he'd never pictured what he'd be doing in the world. Shame was in his heart. He wasn't a man—yet. Sex didn't make him one. Anger didn't make him one. Age didn't make him one. His friends didn't make him one. Manhood wasn't something tangible that one could just slip into like a pair of shoes. Manhood wasn't the bass in his voice. Manhood wasn't defined by the color of one's skin. Manhood was his father sitting next to him. The way he protected and provided, even during times when there was no appreciation from he or Robbie. Manhood was how Lorenzo treated his mother. Manhood was his grandfather. You couldn't act your way into manhood. It was more than being able to plant your feet against the ground or stretch your legs out from a chair to rest atop a table. All this time he'd been searching and rushing to be a man and he had never realized that he'd had the perfect representation all along.

LJ fixed his lips and said the manliest thing he'd ever said, "I want to be like you."

"I'm proud of you son," Betty said as she placed her arm around the neck of LJ. As they sat on the front porch making out the images they saw within the clouds, they reminisced about every hilarious thing LJ did as a child.

"Sixteen!" Betty said with disbelief in her tone.

LJ nodded, smiling at the thought of it. "Yep. Sixteen."

"How's Krystal?" Betty asked.

LJ shrugged his shoulders. "She's fine, I guess. We're back together now."

"*Back* together? I never realized you two *weren't* together.

LJ laughed.

"Ma—can I ask you a question?"

"Sure."

"When you were growing up, what did you think life would be like for you when you became an adult?"

Betty sighed as she sat up in the chair.

"Well, first and foremost the thing that I looked forward to the most was having some *freedom.*" She laughed at the thought and continued, "Boy was I wrong about that one."

"What do you mean?" LJ asked.

"Let's just say there is a word called responsibility that usually puts a cap on whatever type of freedom that lives within your mind."

She took a sip of her tea and continued, "Besides that, I had visions of being a DJ on the radio." She turned to LJ and said, "Why you laughing? I was good at spinning records and I got the voice for it."

"I'm sure you would have been great at it Ma," LJ replied still chuckling at the thought.

"Are you doing anything tonight?" Betty asked.

"I may go see Krystal for a sec, then I'm gonna come on back home."

"Well, you better go now if you going because it's about to storm something nice."

LJ nodded.

Before Betty stood something tugged at her heart. "Come straight home after Krystal's—okay?"

"Yes Ma'am."

"I'm serious LJ. Come straight home. Promise?"

"I promise."

They hug and embraced. Betty held him longer than usual and LJ welcomed it.

Bee lay in bed as Tupac Shakur's song "Trapped" played through his new Walkman. He hadn't left his room since Lorenzo visited two days prior. His room was still dark even when the sun was out. His clothes were still scattered about. The shoebox that was once full of cash was empty now, the smell of marijuana still lingering from it. Trapped is how Bee felt. He was trapped by a situation that would lead him in a direction that was a distant detour from the route he'd envisioned. His visions of escaping the bars of the city to find solace within the game of chess was nothing more than a distant childhood memory or some type of item on a wish list during Christmas, only to learn that Santa wasn't real. Life was. And the odds of him picking its lock or holding on to the innocent lies were no more. Bee was trapped.

With his hands locked together underneath his pillow and his eyes closed, Bee thought a lot about his grandfather and how much he missed him. He imagined the disappointment in his grandfather's eyes if he was alive to see what he'd become. He no longer believed that he was watching down from heaven, because that place didn't exist to Bee anymore. It was becoming harder to make out his grandfather's voice. He often had to look at pictures to remember keen details of his appearance: the redness of his eyes, the way his old skin hung from his face, the way his lips parted when he smiled, the bunch of his brows, the square of his chin. Death and time had a way of doing that—making one forget the better days when life was good. Childhood was a trick, another fallacy tucked under the wings of the gifts of life.

Where would Bee find his solace now? Where would he find his escape when he was trapped within the walls of his truth? The warmth from the handle of the gun was still fresh in his memory. The sight of those young black bodies dropping. The sound of the gun and screams tormenting him like a devil's whisper in the night. The feeling of nothing inside. The taste of sorrow dancing on his tongue.

He'd been ignoring the knocks and distant cries from his mother. Her tears were empty, her words falling on deaf ears. She'd told him she would always be there for him no matter what. She wanted to ease his pain, fix what was broken. But how could one mend a broken heart? He'd seen what a bandage did to pain. The wound would still be there. A temporary fix is what it was and what it would be. Bee was trapped.

Bee opened his eyes as the tape stopped. He removed the headphones from his ears. Dead silence inside, but outside it was alive. He could hear the crickets. The sound of cars whizzing by. Laughter still in the air.

He reached into his pocket and pulled out the chess piece his grandfather had given to him. He placed it near his lips, kissing it softly before gripping it tight within his hand, the same one that had held the gun. His jaws were clenched tight, lips sucked in. He whispered, "I'm sorry, Grandpa," before tossing the chess piece into the pile of clothing and liter that covered his floor.

Standing at his door, he turned and stared into his room as if he was foreshadowing it would be his last. It would become a distant memory, and he wouldn't have a picture to help him make out the empty spaces within it. Childhood lost.

The sky was a purple hue as a streak of lightning bolted across it. The crackle and rumble of the thunder caused a nearby car alarm to go off. Clouds were breaking open as a shower of rain fell from the sky. Kids scampered and ran for shelter. One young boy trying to jump a ramp into his yard missed the ramp and hit the curb, causing him to superman into his yard. This caused a curl to form on Bee's lips. He watched two young kids, Cedric and Larry, race in the street as the rain danced on their frames.

He sat atop the trunk of his father's car under the carport, hand deep into a bag of chips. The darkness that was inside him was illuminated by life on the outside. He returned a wave from a neighbor holding a newspaper over her head as she ran inside. He wiped his hands along his thighs, freeing them from the crumbs. He turned his head to see a dark brown car turn the corner, the window tint blocking any view inside. The car slowed as it approached Bee's house. Bee froze, no longer knowing how to move his limbs. The streets had taught him this level of paranoia. There was no safety net to life.

The car stopped. The window rolled down slowly. Bee remained still. His eyes watching, awaiting his fate. A familiar face appeared over the window. The door opened and a young man walked up the driveway. The young man was Travis.

The voice of the street was often loud. Its reach and influence stretching like one's shadow. There was no escaping it. Bee and Travis stood, both timid in their words and actions. "You know that wasn't us—right?" Travis said in that familiar tone that Bee once knew to be true. He'd went on to tell Bee that the night he had gotten jumped was not at the hands of him nor Freddie nor Ant. Travis would tell Bee that he'd tried to silence the situation for days at a time only to find his reach at a dead-end from Bee avoiding him. He went on to tell Bee that he'd never faulted he nor LJ for what happened at Southbrook Mall. He'd known how tall they stood. He'd known LJ was protected, but he wasn't a snitch. He went on to express his hurt at losing two friends in the span of two months. Travis asked Bee about chess. He asked Bee about life. Then he asked Bee the hardest question that escaped his lips that night. He asked Bee if he'd had anything to do with the death of their friend Freddie. The voice of the streets was loud, and the streets had been talking.

Bee allowed his eyes to catch Travis'. No words escaped his lips. His face said it all. His eyes held the truth that Travis hoped was a lie. He knew the boys that Bee had started running with. He knew the strength of their reach, the pull of their influence—the violence that would follow.

Silence fell over them as they stared out into the rainfall, a flurry of drops bouncing against the concrete.

"What you gonna do, Bee?" Travis asked.

Bee hunched his shoulders before dropping his head. That emptiness that he'd felt before walking outside had returned. The feeling of the unknown.

"This is so fucked up," Travis added. "You know what comes behind this right?" he asked, his voice cracking in a quiet whisper. "You remember how we used to play ball in the rain?" Travis continued, cracking a smile.

Bee nodded. "Yeah, we would play for hours."

"I remember when me, you, LJ and Zoe would get into mad shit when we were younger," Travis said, eyes gazing into the street.

"Most of the time it was you getting us into stuff, because you were older," Bee replied, and a small snigger fell from his mouth.

Travis began to laugh a little harder. Bee stared him down with curious eyes and asked, "What's so funny?"

"I just thought about that time when I made you and LJ smoke that paper that y'all thought was weed. All day y'all was talking about how high y'all was, knowing damn well you niggas wasn't high."

Bee smiled. "Nigga—we *was* high. It was probably from the ink on the paper."

They both laughed some more before silence fell. It was as if at that precise moment they knew things would never be the same.

"Fo' life, right?" Travis said, looking into Bee's eyes before extending his hand for a pound.

Bee lifted his head and looked at Travis before nodding. Two boys under the age of twenty talking about the wages of life and death as if they were men on the edge of their death beds, neither realizing that the streets were a trap. The entrapment felt by many like them was created by design, but it had since become stitched into the realm of their reality. Art imitated life and life imitated art. The truth no longer mattered because it had been erased generations before them. They were playing a game with a fixed result—a true form of entrapment.

FREEDOM

The city was quiet. Night had fallen. Tears from heaven no longer fell from the sky. It was darker than usual. The sky was a deep black, no mixture of hues illuminating it. Power outages worked their way throughout the Low Reign, making eyes narrow, brows pinch tight and kids blow out their jaws. Families sat and stared at blank televisions, candles lit. Some sat on porches in silence, being respectful of God's work. Fathers slept through it. Mothers worried. Kids watched the streets from windows, wishing they could be outside. A rumble of thunder every couple of minutes would put some on alert that another storm was brewing. One could smell it in the air: the dampness, thick musk, bitter aroma.

LJ, sitting on the curb, legs stretched into the street, swatted away pesky mosquitos. In his hand was the gift his father had given him at the dinner table. He shook it again, placing it close to his ear, squinting his eyes in full concentration, his mind wondering and curiosity at the tip of his tongue.

"Just open it already," Krystal said, twirling the piece of gum that was extended from her mouth. She'd always been the antsy type when it came to special days when she was expecting a gift. The twinkle of her eyes, the butterflies in her stomach and the exuberant jolt of energy running through her frame would send her spinning, guessing and hoping that whatever was in the wrapped gift would be something she would cherish forever.

"Can't. Not until tomorrow," LJ replied. "Promised my dad."

"What do you think it is?" Krystal asked, followed by an enlarging pink bubble ballooning from her lips. Through a slightly open mouth as she blew life into the air pocket of the gum.

LJ shrugged his shoulders.

"*So*—Mr. Sixteen, what you got planned for tomorrow? Party? *Hanging* out with the boys?" Krystal said, leaning heavily to the right, arms tucked and folded against her chest, trying to find some bass in her voice to mimic how LJ talked amongst his friends.

LJ laughed and nudged her against the shoulder before replying. "Not sure yet." He placed the box back into his pocket. He shook his head. "I thought I'd feel different, you know? More grown. But honestly, I still feel the same."

"So, *what*—you just thought you were just gonna magically change?" Krystal asked, stretching her neck away from LJ, eyes at full bloom. Voice back at her sweet natural tone.

"I don't know what I thought." LJ lowered his head and mouthed, "At least not anymore."

Krystal rubbed her hands over her bare arms and stared into the night. She heard the chirp of the crickets and felt the stings from the mosquitos. No cars had passed by. She scooted closer to LJ, arm to arm.

"What's really bothering you?" she asked. "You've been kinda down."

LJ rubbed his hand over his head. "I don't know. I just feel weird, ya know."

"Weird how?"

"I don't know. That's what I mean. I really don't know."

"It might just be the storm," Krystal replied. She closed her eyes and took a deep inhale, taking in the dampness, musk and bitter aroma. "My dad always says that our actions mirror either the weather or music."

"*What*—your dad is some kinda philosopher now?"

Krystal nudged LJ on the shoulder, a crooked smile on her face. "Quit playing. My dad knows what he be talking about."

"Your dad seems cool," LJ replied.

"You and your dad still fighting?" Krystal asked, her eyes serious.

LJ shook his head. "Naw—we cool now."

A voice echoed and called, "Krystal, time to come in. It's getting late."

LJ looked at his watch as he stood from his feet. "Damn. I didn't realize it was this late. I need to head home too before my mom rolls up over here and starts embarrassing me."

Krystal's smile turned to laughter. They gazed into each other's eyes, neither wanting to say goodbye. Krystal tilted her head to the side, eyes still locked with LJ's. "*So*—do we go together again?"

LJ extended his hands toward Krystal's. A rumble of thunder made them look toward the sky as a streak of lighting flashed, adding a golden blue to the darkness. "I guess so," LJ replied with playful banter in his tone.

"You better know so," Krystal said returning the playfulness.

They hugged under the night and kissed cheeks. LJ feared her shotgun-toting military father. He didn't want to risk her father seeing him kissing his daughter in the night. His lips against hers, tight, slow, mouth opened... He feared her dad would snap like those crazed ex-military folks he'd seen on the television once. His body would be riddled with bullets as Krystal stood over him, screaming "What did you do!" at her dad.

"Tomorrow!" Krystal whispered into his ear, letting her bottom lip graze against his ear lobe—the best way she knew how to be seductive.

"Tomorrow," LJ replied before he walked into the night and she could no longer see his frame. She smiled as she stood in her yard, bare feet against the wet lawn. She only heard the crickets chirping and the intensity and regularity of the rumbling of thunder. Another storm was coming.

LJ, jogging home, felt drops of rain tap against his head and skin. The smell of it was more intense. He increased his pace. His eyes caught two kids on a bicycle, one on the seat, the other sitting atop the handlebars. He jogged past the stench of marijuana, laughter cutting through the night, more thunder, car alarms, playful screams, music. Some areas were quiet, mostly where the older people stayed. He jogged past the graffitied stop sign, boys on the corner, men talking under the carport, a couple complaining about the power being out, a lady screaming at her cheating spouse, a kid wailing in the background. LJ continued to jog. As he approached his block, he stopped, gasping for air. The rain had come to a stop, but a shower was coming.

His eyes caught sight of the old burgundy car that was long in the back under Bee's carport. As he got closer, he could focus in and see a set of skinny black legs dangling off the back of it. It was Bee.

"I know where *you* coming from nigga!" Bee yelled from across the street.

LJ turned and began his jog toward Bee, flashing a smile at his friend. "Nigga—where you been? I've been trying to get at you forever."

Bee no longer sported the curl he used to. He'd since shaved it off. He now wore a low, close, even cut over his scalp. He was leaner in the face, harder in a way. His lips had darkened at the bottom with spots of pink at the top due to his increased smoking habit. The scar across his face was still visible. He looked like his father Charles.

"I just been chillin'—you know," Bee replied.

LJ hopped atop the hood with his friend. He studied his face briefly before breaking his gaze into the street. Both he and Bee sat in silence as their legs dangled from the car, swinging into the night, each trying to find the words to say.

"You wanna hit this bud with me?" Bee asked as he opened his hand, exposing the freshly rolled paper joint resting in his palm.

LJ shook his head. "Naw, man. I'm cool. Do you though!"

Bee hunched his shoulders and replied, "Aite then." He hopped from the car, reached inside an empty flowerpot and pulled out a lighter. "Let's walk around the corner real quick. I don't want Moms to come out here trippin' and shit."

LJ looked at his watch and up the street toward his house. He was calculating how long it would take them to walk around the corner and back. He didn't want to miss his curfew. He wanted to show his parents that he could be responsible. He wanted to show them that he would be different at sixteen. Even though he had more to learn, he at least understood some aspects of manhood: being true to your word.

LJ hopped off the car and followed Bee down the driveway. They stood in the middle of the street as Bee lit his joint. Bee's face was scrunched up as he took the first hit, coughing as his eyes turned red and watered, like the men they'd grown up watching over the years. LJ thought about the days when Bee wouldn't dare raise a joint to his lips. LJ had always been the one to try things first and talk Bee into it. Bee took two subtle hits and extended his hand to LJ. LJ declined again.

"Just being generous nigga," Bee said as he shrugged his shoulders. They both broke into a laugh.

"Mane I can't believe I'm gonna be sixteen tomorrow," LJ said, smile across his face.

"I know you can't nigga," Bee replied, smoke falling from his mouth. "What you got going on tomorrow?"

"I don't know yet. We might do the usual to start. You *know*—breakfast and shit like that."

Bee nodded. "Power must be back on." Their eyes caught the sight of life as light and the glare from televisions could be seen inside windows.

"It's about damn time," LJ replied. "Now I can call Krystal when I get to the crib."

"I knew that's where yo' ass was coming from," Bee said as smoke curled across his lips.

"We just got back together," LJ replied, taking in the contact smoke from the joint.

"It's about to storm like a bitch. I can smell it," Bee said. "My pops told me he knows how to smell the rain in the air. I didn't believe him at first until that nigga was right."

"How is he?" LJ asked, almost a whisper.

Bee hunched his shoulders. "I ain't talk to the nigga."

Silence cut between them before LJ asked, "Yo, I saw my dad at your crib awhile back. What did he want?"

Bee blew more smoke from his mouth before reaching into his pocket to pull out a cigarette. His eyes were now reddened, lids heavier. His words were louder, harder in the vowels. He shook his head. "Ain't nothing. Just questions and shit."

More awkward silence cut between them.

"I be hearing shit," LJ said straight, no smiles. Seriousness about the eyes.

"What kinda shit?" Bee asked, smoke blowing from his flared nostrils.

"Nigga I ain't gotta say," LJ said, stopping his strut. "I know why you been staying away and shit. We been cool since forever. I know."

Bee nodded. "Mane you remember when we used to race these shits?" Bee asked, holding the cigarette butt in his hand and abruptly changing the conversation like the old drunks did that stood outside the liquor store.

LJ allowed a smile to break the seriousness in his face. He had flashbacks of the memory Bee had resonated. The two of them: he, round in the face, fat clinging to his bones, and Bee—skinny and frail—always looking for the next adventure. The two of them learning life together, the falsehoods of manhood, the trials of the street, how to smell the rain in the air.

LJ saw a police car fly by from a distance. He looked at his watch and figured it must be his dad. He envisioned him walking inside, thanking the Lord for allowing him to make it home. He would take his hand and rub it over Robbie's head. He would then walk over to Betty to smack her lightly across her backside before planting a kiss to her lips. She would call him 'Egyptian eyes' and they would whisper adult things to each other that would make Robbie cover his ears.

Bee tossed the cigarette butt in a field of weeds and overgrown grass. He no longer thought about whether he was a weed or a flower. The guilt that had been suppressing him was starting to subside. It had almost normalized, like his friend in the red hat had said it would. He was just playing the hand life had dealt him. He was a pawn on the board, making one step at a time. Each step leading to what could become a fatal mistake. Lorenzo had asked Bee about what happened the night those three boys were shot, leaving one dead. There was no proof to link Bee to the crime. There were no witnesses, but the streets knew. He'd went on to tell Bee not to involve LJ into any of his shit. He told Bee to get his shit together. He told him that he believed in him and there would always be a seat at his table for him whenever he wanted to come. He told him to reach out to his father, learn from him and understand his actions, so that he could avoid them.

"Ready to head back?" Bee said. "You *know*—to meet your curfew and shit."

"Let's take this short cut," LJ said, looking past the weeds and overgrown grass in the field.

"Aite," Bee replied.

"Race?" LJ asked.

"What?" Bee asked, disfiguring his face. "Nigga I ain't about to run through no fucking wet ass grass and I know you ain't trying to fuck up your sneaks."

LJ shrugged his shoulders and looked down at his feet. "Fuck it. Let's race for old times' sake. *What*? Scared I'm gonna smoke yo' ass?"

Bee, face still scrunched up, replied, "*What*? Nigga you must be smoking crack if you think yo' ass can beat me."

"Let's do it then."

Bee reached down to tighten his shoestrings as they

both wore the same smiles on their faces as they had when they were just kids in the street looking for their next boyhood adventure. Just as Bee stood to break into a runner's pose, a car pulled up and someone yelled out some words which were soon followed by that deafening sound of gun fire.

Bee was gasping for air as he leaped over fences, his feet pounding as he trudged through the wet grass and mud, splashing puddles, leaving his mark. His heart was racing, rising to his throat. Bee didn't want to die. He had a lot to live for and at that point he realized it, so he ran for his life. He could hear LJ's feet behind his, pounding and trudging through the wet grass and mud, splashing puddles, leaving his mark too. He could hear the quick pants of his breath. LJ's gasps. He could hear the strain of their voices as they leaped, climbed and ran, until he realized that his feet pounding against the grass were the only ones he'd heard. He stopped, bent over his knees, turned to see that his friend was no longer there.

Something inside Betty struck her core at 9:13 that evening. She had been lying down, book facedown over her chest, eyes closed, waiting for LJ to return home by 9:30. She wasn't awakened by the sound of the door or by Lorenzo and his kiss atop her forehead.

She wasn't awakened by Robbie asking his dad if they could wrestle before he got ready for bed. She wasn't awakened by the sound of the television when the power had come back on. She was only awakened by that eerie jolt that ran through her body. She rose up, gasping for air. Her amber, cat-like eyes were open at full bloom before a tear broke from one of them for no reason at all. She felt her grip on keeping her kids from the street loosen. She heard the whisper of God telling her to wake up. She felt a piece of her heart tear, her soul wither.

Outside, people walked to the edge of their driveways, some looking out of windows, others chatting on their phones and many doing nothing at all because their ears and eyes had become accustomed to the sound. As the bass in God's voice vibrated the sky, it opened a strong shower of rainfall.

That night, when people learned about what happened, many cried, asked why, shook their heads, prayed and cursed, anger in their bones. The people of the Low Reign felt that dark cloud rise above them again. The following morning there would be clean-up Saturdays in some households. There would be boys trying to stretch out of their boyish skin, fitting themselves for manhood. Life would go on in the Low

Reign. The people would find their smile and joy again. They were a strong and prideful people, a people of truth and vulnerability amid the strength of the generational curses that rode their backs. They were survivors.

Made in the USA
Middletown, DE
08 September 2019